AF581079

By Cara Bastone

Ready or Not
Promise Me Sunshine
No Matter What

LOVE LINES SERIES

Call Me Maybe
Sweet Talk
Seatmate

Seatmate

Seatmate

A Novel

CARA BASTONE

THE DIAL PRESS
NEW YORK

The Dial Press
An imprint of Random House
A division of Penguin Random House LLC
1745 Broadway, New York, NY 10019
randomhousebooks.com
penguinrandomhouse.com

A Dial Press Trade Paperback Original

Originally published as an Audible Original by Audible and subsequently in a digital edition in the United Kingdom by Headline Eternal, an imprint of Headline Publishing Group in 2022.

This book contains an excerpt from the forthcoming book *Through the Blue* by Cara Bastone. This excerpt has been set for this edition only and may not reflect the final content of the forthcoming edition.

ISBN 979-8-217-19957-0

Printed in the United States of America

1st Printing

BOOK TEAM: Production editor: Cindy Berman • Managing editor: Leah Sims • Production manager: Linnea Knollmueller

The authorized representative in the EU for product safety and compliance is Penguin Random House Ireland, Morrison Chambers, 32 Nassau Street, Dublin D02 YH68, Ireland. https://eu-contact.penguin.ie

For Jon, the best seatmate of my life. Thank you for giving me a reason to take all those Megabus rides from Boston to New York. And for Mishi, the second best seatmate. Thanks for giving us a reason to finally get a car.

Chapter One

"Excuse me, miss. Hi. Is this seat taken?"

"Nope. All yours if you want it."

"Thanks!"

"So . . . I take it literally every other seat was already occupied on the bus?"

"How'd you guess?"

"I honestly can't think of another reason why someone would electively choose the aisle seat in the back row directly across from a bus bathroom."

"Yeah . . . probably should have gotten here a few minutes earlier. I'm just glad I didn't miss the bus."

"Well, here we go."

"Bye, Boston."

"In this traffic, I think you're going to have at least another hour to say goodbye to Boston."

"Right. Uh . . . You know, it helps if you don't think of it as traffic. Just imagine that the bus is legally obligated to drive all the way to New York at thirty miles per hour. That way it's a lot less frustrating."

"Ah, I see the logic in that. Just surrender to what you can't control."

"Precisely."

"I'm Gwen, by the way."

"Hi, Gwen. I'm Sam."

"Nice to meetcha."

"Yes, um. You too."

"I like your hair."

"Oh. Yeah. Thanks. It's new. The indigo part, I mean. The brown part is the same as always."

"You don't see a lot of indigo hair."

"Yeah. The hairstylist was very excited when I asked for it."

"Oh, you went to a stylist? That's why it looks so neat and tidy. Most people dye their hair interesting colors while they're kneeling over their bathtub, trying not to dye their fingers the same color."

"Ha, yeah? Sounds like you have some personal experience with that?"

"I would argue that dyeing your hair an unflattering shade of red is actually a really productive and healthy way to get through a break-up. Maybe even a rite of passage."

"Ah."

"Is that why you dyed yours? Rebellion after an overbearing ex?"

"Huh? Oh, definitely not. No. I guess I just thought, um, time for a change? I got it done on Friday and they haven't seen it at work yet. So, I guess we'll see tomorrow morning if I have to shave it all off."

"Oh, I hope you don't shave it! Just dye it back if you have to. It would be a shame to lose all that hair. You've got a very . . . Pepé Le Pew thing going on. Except, your stripe is indigo not white."

"Oh, brother. That is definitely not what I was going for with this hairstyle."

"Skunk who can't take a hint isn't the vibe you were going for? How odd."

"Yeah, no. Pepé was a twerp. Is he even still on the air?

I hope not. His whole *no means yes* thing is just creepy when you think about it."

"Agreed. He had great hair though."

"Oh. Sorry about the annoying ringtone. I should probably . . ."

"No worries, go ahead."

"Hey, Ma . . . Yup, I made it. Sorry, I should have texted you . . . Already on the I-95 . . . Uh huh . . . Uh huh . . . Uh huh . . . No, you didn't. Are you serious? Hold on, let me . . . Oh, a tuna-fish sandwich and a hard-boiled egg. Thanks, Ma. That was sweet of you . . . Yes, I'm buckled. I swear. Did you call Aunt Laura yet? . . . Well, you'll feel better when you do . . . Uh huh . . . Uh huh . . . Uh huh . . . Well, it's rude to talk on the phone on the bus, so I'll call you when I get in . . . Don't worry, it'll be fine . . . Love you too. Bye. Ahem. Ah, sorry about that."

"No problem at all. Your mom?"

"Yup."

"She seems caring."

"She is. Maybe a little too much? But, anyhow. Don't worry."

"Hm?"

"I'm not going to eat a tuna-fish sandwich and a hard-boiled egg on an enclosed bus."

"*Oh, thank God*. I think my life flashed before my eyes."

"Yeah, that's my mother for ya. Sweet enough to pack you a secret lunch, unbothered enough to pack the stinkiest foods known to mankind."

"Look, I know it's lunchtime, but if you can choke down a hard-boiled egg while sitting across from a Megabus bathroom then you deserve some kind of medal. Seriously, I wouldn't even be mad. I'd be impressed."

"Speaking of the bathroom, I think we have an incoming."

"Oh, boy. Quick, let's talk about something else."

"So that we're not thinking about whatever is happening in there?"

"Exactly."

"Um . . . Um . . . I'm terrible at thinking of topics."

"So, your mother is in Boston, but you work in New York?"

"Oh. Yes. Correct."

"And you live in New York?"

"Also correct. She's lived in the Boston area her whole life. I moved to New York for undergrad and never left."

"Which borough do you live in?"

"Queens. Sunnyside."

"Oh, that's a great neighborhood."

"You've spent time there?"

"I've spent time in every borough."

"So . . . NYC is home for you too, then?"

"Yes. No. Sort of. Ugh. Sorry, let me check this text."

"Bad news?"

"Huh? Oh. Not really. Just this guy, he's sort of my work rival and every so often he taunts me over text."

"He's . . . a grown man?"

"Uh. Yeah?"

"And he's taunting you over text? What an ass."

"Yeah, I wish it were more complicated than that, but pretty much you just hit the nail on the head."

"So, hold on . . . What does *yes, no, sort of* mean?"

"Hm?"

"Is New York not home for you?"

"Oh. Well, I travel for work so I don't really spend enough time at my apartment to think of it as home. But yeah, New York generally is home. I moved there right after high school as well. So, where did you go to school?"

"Hunter. What's your job, then? That requires so much travel?"

"I'm a photographer. And a writer. And you?"

"Oh, wow. That's *so* cool. Do you work for a magazine or something?"

"I freelance. And can usually get an article or two in my buddy's lifestyle magazine. But for the most part I run a blog."

"A blog? Cool. How would I find it?"

"Oh . . . you want to see it?"

"Definitely."

"Ah. Here. I can pull it up on my phone."

"Holy smokes, Gwen, these photos are gorgeous. Do you mostly focus on jewelry?"

"Well, my main interests lie in how and why people choose to decorate themselves in general. Often that's jewelry. But it's also tattoos, fashion, protective gear, hairstyles, you name it."

"Ah. Hence your interest in my hair."

"Well, it *is* pretty interesting hair. About that, actually—"

"So, you meet people, photograph them and their . . . decoration choices and then write about them?"

"Yeah, I do long interviews with them. Sometimes I end up spending a whole day, or even a few days with them, depending on how well we hit it off. But I find that it's usually a great entry point into getting someone talking about themselves. Why they dress the way they do or why that particular tattoo in that particular place or 'this was my mother's locket that she gave me on her deathbed and I've never taken it off,' that kind of thing. Oh, shhh! *I think they're coming out of the bathroom!*"

"Wow."

"Don't look up. Just ignore it. Stay focused on this space here, between us. Whatever happens over there does not concern us, Sam."

"Right, right. The bathroom eighteen inches to my left does not exist. Okay, um, in the interest of distraction: question. And if it's too impertinent, feel free to tell me to shove it."

"Okay . . ."

"Because, seriously, it really might not be any of my business."

"Uh huh."

"But this is where my mind automatically goes when I hear about someone with a job like yours. And I know that might mean I'm a really . . . boring person, but yeah."

"What's the question?"

"Oh! Right. Well, how, exactly, do you make money?"

"Ah, of course. The age-old question. Moolah. Well, when I was first getting started, I was usually able to find waitressing work wherever I went. Which was actually a really great way to meet people to interview. I worked as a tour guide once, though that was a disaster because I was more interested in hearing about the people's lives than I was in telling them about what they were looking at. Then when things started picking up and I got better at both photography and writing, like I said, I got the occasional article in my friend's mag. That helped make ends meet a little. But now there's enough traffic on my blog that I sell ad space."

"Wow. You must be really successful, then."

"Well, moderately successful. I usually make just enough to be able to cover my next trip to somewhere else. You are really good at getting someone talking, by the way. I never usually go into such detail."

"Ha. Wow. Definitely no one has ever said that to me before. I guess I'm just genuinely interested. So . . . do you have one? A next trip lined up?"

"I'm hoping, *hoping*, that in a month or so I'll be in Portugal if I can get the money to work out. But I'll have to land this big project."

"*Portugal*. Wow."

"Have you been there?"

"No. I've never actually left the States. Barely even left the East Coast, to be honest. My mother's not a great traveler and I spend a lot of time with her, so when I'm using vacation days we're usually in the Boston area together. Aaaaaand, right about now is when I wish I was really good at lying. Because then maybe I wouldn't have just admitted to a world-traveling photographer and writer that I pretty much use up all my vacation days at a knit shop helping my mom pick out her next project. Just pretend I said something way cooler than that, please."

"It doesn't sound uncool to me."

"You're joking, right?"

"I mean . . . I guess it's uncool if you say it is. But . . . there's nothing inherently wrong with knitting shops. And besides, I don't think you're terrible at lying. You lied to your mother."

"When?"

"You told her you were buckled in."

"Oh. Right. I mean, do these things even have seat belts?"

"Of course not. But your mother doesn't know that."

"She's been trying for years to get me to move back to Boston, so I think finding out that there aren't any seat belts on the Megabus I take once a month to see her might push her over the edge."

"You take this trip once a month? Good Lord, you must have an incredibly high pain tolerance."

"Like I said, as long as you can dissociate from the pace of the traffic it's not so bad. Oh. And noise canceling headphones help a lot."

"Oh. Am I keeping you from your headphones? Sorry. By all means, plug in. I can totally occupy myself over here."

"Oh, ah—Shoot, sorry. That's my mom calling again. Let me just . . ."

"Go ahead."

"Hey, Ma . . . Yup. 95. For a long time . . . Oh, good, you talked to Aunt Laura . . . Uh huh . . . Wait. No. Ma . . . No. No, I really don't want—Do I really have to remind you how bad the last blind date was? Puke, Ma, there was *puke* involved . . . I don't want you and Aunt Laura to set me up again . . . I'm sure she's great but—Oh fine. Just give me her number and I'll—*What?* What do you mean she's *meeting me at the bus stop*?! That's . . . that's . . . I actually have no words . . . This is . . . I can't . . . *Ma* . . . Look, I'm in public right now. I don't want to fight about this, but you need to fix this immediately. Call this woman up and tell her not to meet me at the bus stop! I have to go. Love you."

"Um. Wow?"

"Urghhhhhhhh. I can't believe that just happened."

"So . . ."

"Any chance you didn't actually hear all of that?"

"We're sitting next to one another. So yeah. I heard all of that."

"Honey, even I heard that too, from one row up.
And a little word from the wise? Cut her loose."

"How am I supposed to cut her loose? I don't even have her number!"

"No, not the blind date. Your mother!"

"I can't cut my mother loose. She's my mother. But yes. Point taken. I could probably stand to answer the phone a little less. Here. I'll just put it on silent. Oh, she just texted me. Oh, my God. Look what she wrote, Gwen."

"It says: *She'll be there by seven. Don't worry, I already warned her about your hair.*"

"God grant me strength to deal with my mother."

"Your mother is stone cold, son. Good luck."

"What's your name, ma'am? I'm Gwen and this is Sam."

"I'm Shirley. Nice to meet you both. I'm going back to my program, but if there are any more updates on the blind date, give me a poke."

"You got it, Shirley."

"Nice to meet you, Shirley. Oh, Gwen, there's another text."

"Read it out loud to me. I'm getting motion sick from reading."

"It says: *She's a good Catholic girl from Scituate. Planning on moving home from New York around Christmastime. Fourth-grade teacher. Wear deodorant, honey.*"

"Do ya often skip deodorant, Sam?"

"No! And definitely not when I'm going to be sitting next to a stranger on a bus."

"Much appreciated. At least you have that going for you when you meet the woman of your dreams in just a few hours."

"What makes you think she's the woman of my dreams?"

"Um, according to your mother she's a good Catholic girl from Scituate? She sounds lovely."

"Sure. And she's a fourth-grade teacher who's moving back to the Boston area by Christmas. It's like my mother selected her from a mail-order catalogue."

"Sam, your mother has gone out of her way to find the perfect person for you to immediately settle down and spend the rest of your life with. Yet, for some strange reason, you sound less than enthused."

"Imagine that."

"A non-consensual blind date set up by your mom isn't how you envisioned meeting your dream girl? How odd."

"Maybe, *maybe*, if this was the first time, I might take it more seriously."

"She makes a habit of drop-kicking you into blind dates?"

"This makes . . . seven? Eight?"

"Woof."

"Yeah."

"And the last one involved puke?"

"Preceded by quite a bit of binge drinking. Hers. Not mine. It's not like any of these dates have ever gone well. But that one was a particular low."

"Your mother is zero for eight? Really? There hasn't been a single good date amongst all of them?"

"If I'm being honest . . . I don't think that's her fault. It's not like every single one of those women were duds. I mean, none of them were duds. The binge-drinker was clearly going through something at the time and we weren't a match. But for the most part they were all really nice people."

"So . . . what was the problem, then? You just can't bring yourself to date someone your mom has pre-selected?"

"No, no, it's not that . . . I don't think. It's more that *I'm* the problem . . . I've recently come to the conclusion that I'm a spectacularly bad date."

"Wait, really?"

"Yeah."

"Do you have any examples you'd like to share with the class?"

"Ummmm. Well, remember how I said I'm bad at thinking of topics?"

"Sure."

"Well, I wasn't lying. There will be a silence on a date and I'll think to myself, '*This silence is lasting too long, you should think of something to say, Sam.*' But then all I can think about is how long the silence is lasting. And how it's getting longer and longer and then pretty soon she's sighing and looking out the window or checking her phone."

"And the 'she' in this scenario just makes you dangle there? Rude!"

"No, no, usually this is like the fifth or sixth time this has happened over the course of a single meal. When I say I can never think of topics, I mean I can *never* think of topics."

"Oh. Well, yeah, that can definitely make a first date . . . stilted. Anything else?"

"I get very awkward about paying."

"Ah. You like to go halvsies on a date?"

"I like to do whatever *she* wants to do. If she wants me to buy her dinner, great! Wonderful! I figure it's the least I can do considering *my* mother is the reason we're on the date in the first place. But I've learned that some women don't like it if you pay for everything because then they feel beholden and they'd rather split the meal. And some would prefer that we itemize out the check and pay for exactly what we each ordered."

"Really?"

"Yeah. I've seen it all. But that also leads me to the next thing that makes me a weird date."

"I'm all ears."

"In order to anticipate the potential check-splitting or itemization mayhem, I usually just order exactly what she orders."

"What?"

"Yeah, that way, if she wants to split the check or itemize it, then we've gotten the exact same thing and it's easy to split everything down the middle."

"So, if she orders plain pasta, no sauce, and a side salad, no dressing, and tap water . . ."

"That's exactly what I order."

"But say she wants filet mignon, a glass of their most expensive red, and three desserts . . ."

"That one has played out almost exactly like that, actually. It nearly bankrupted me, but it was a delicious meal."

"And you have no preferences?"

"Of course I have preferences! I just . . . ignore them for the night."

"And this doesn't weird these women out?"

"Um, some of them think it's a compliment, as if they've discovered the best things on the menu and I just had to follow their lead. And yes, some of them think it's very weird."

"So basically, you don't talk on these dates, you order identical meals, down to the very last candlestick, and then you attempt to read her mind about the bill."

"Yup."

"Yeah, Sam, I've gotta admit, these sound like kinda bad dates."

"I'm telling you."

"And this dinner thing, it's the only card up your sleeve? You never go to the movies or an art exhibit or to see the Christmas lights or a show or something?"

"Well, yes, I've done stuff like that on *other* dates. Just not on these blind dates. Blind dates are a different animal! Have you ever been on one before?"

"Have I ever been on a blind date? Ummmm."

"Hold that thought, sorry, she's calling me again."

"Go ahead."

"Ma? Hi. Look, I'm going to ask you one more time, please just cancel on this woman. I really don't—Wait. What? Are you serious? . . . No. You're joking. How did you . . .? Doesn't she live in Seattle? Last I heard she was married . . . Divorced . . . Wow . . . I . . . Ma . . . Are you there? We're going through a bad reception zone. I'll have to call you later . . . I'll think about it, okay? Love you."

"You look like you just got some interesting news."

"Huh?"

"You've gone very pale and your eyes look like they've

forgotten how to close. There you go, good job. Blink blink. Get some oxygen to those puppies."

"My mother got me a date with Katie McConnick."

"Who is Katie McConnick?"

"My high-school crush."

"Wow."

"Yeah."

"And she arranged it for a bus station? Does it get any more meet-cutey than that? *Sam!* This is so exciting!"

"How the hell did she arrange a date with Katie McConnick?"

"So, Katie McConnick is the nice Catholic girl who wants to move back to the Boston area?"

"I guess so. My mother said she was going to keep it a surprise, but then she got spooked when I was being so stubborn about not wanting to go on the date, so she told me."

"Sam?"

"Hm?"

"I gotta say. You look a little green around the gills."

"Do I?"

"I can't tell, is this Katie McConnick thing a good thing or a bad thing?"

"I mean . . . Did you ever have a high-school crush?"

"Sure. Matt Judd. Mohawk, Slayer T-shirts, the whole nine. Total hottie."

"So did anything happen with him?"

"We fooled around in the utility closet at Homecoming, but he called me a tease when I didn't want to go further. My crush dried up pretty fast."

"Wait, seriously? What an asshole."

"Actually, I ran into him a few years ago at a bar in Brooklyn and he apologized. He said it's something that's bothered him for a long time and he always felt bad about it. He wanted me to know that he'd liked me for a long time but that he had this stupid idea that girls liked mean guys, so he was trying to fit that persona."

"Wow. He said all that?"

"Sure did. We're not friends really, but I would be happy to see him if I ever ran into him again. What happened with you and Katie McConnick?"

"Pretty much the opposite of that."

"The opposite of making out in a utility closet?"

"Yeah. I watched from afar while other guys were brave enough to take her to dances and, presumably, make out in utility closets."

"But you never asked her?"

"I barely ever even got up the courage to talk to her."

"Oh, no."

"Yeah. Except, we worked together on a two-person project once. It was a history project. We had to make a 3D map of one of the battles in the civil war."

"Wow. You still remember the subject matter and everything?"

"It was the only time I was ever able to talk to her without doing an impression of a chipmunk, so yeah, it kind of stuck in my head."

"Well, what happened with the project? You didn't get close enough to tell her how you felt?"

"Definitely not. We always worked on the project at her house because her dad was an elementary-school art teacher so he had tons of extra supplies for us to work on the map, but that also meant that—"

"Her dad was always around."

"Pretty much, yeah. But that's just an excuse. I don't think I ever even had any intention of telling her how I felt. Or hinting. Way too scary."

"So you never confessed your feelings."

"Not even close."

"Have you ever confessed your feelings to anyone else you've had a crush on?

"Well, sure . . ."

"Do I hear a 'but' in there?"

"I think you're going to tell me it doesn't count."

"Why wouldn't it count?"

"Because now that I really think about it, I think I've only told people about my feelings *after* we've already started dating."

"Ah, I see. You've done the whole *we're hanging out and hooking up and dating around* thing. And then further down the line, once all that's established, you tell them how you feel."

"Is that bad?"

"No! Not at all. That can be really nice. It just . . . It just doesn't quite have the cathartic release of telling someone how you feel *before* all that happens. When everything is on the line and the whole point is that those kinds of feelings curl up and die a resentful little death if you never act on them. So, you *have* to speak them out loud."

"I . . . take it that you've confessed your feelings before?"

"Yes. It was both terrible and wonderful."

"How so?"

"Oh, he didn't feel the same way I did. He said I was really great, but that he wasn't in a place to want to really be in a romantic relationship with anyone. This was maybe . . . six or seven years ago? So, that was hard. But the truth is, once I told him how I felt and got a definite answer in return, all those feelings didn't have to stay cooped up inside me anymore. I just let them out. And pretty soon, they were gone. I felt totally released from the whole thing. And I watched as other girls got tangled up with him. They'd do the whole *kiss-kiss-are-we-gonna-be-something-more* thing, and nothing ever came of those hook-ups. I knew that would have been me too, if I hadn't told him how I felt immediately. He knew not to mess around with me because I'd been honest and he didn't want to hurt me."

"So . . . even though you didn't end up together, you still count that as a good experience?"

"Definitely. I feel really proud of it now, even though it hurt. I was brave."

"Why are all your stories cooler than all of my stories?"

"Huh? What do you mean?"

"Nothing. I just . . . let me think . . . what's something super impressive that I've done that I can casually brag about?"

"I wasn't casually bragging!"

"No, you weren't. You were just honestly telling me a story, which is what makes it even cooler."

"You have a chance to be very cool in just a few hours."

"With Katie?"

"Yes! Are you kidding me? You have a date with an old crush in just a few hours. You're finally gonna get your resolution. And it'll be that much sweeter because it's been so many years in the making."

"Hmm. Maybe."

"You don't sound convinced."

"If you were Katie . . ."

"Okay . . ."

"And you were waiting at the bus station for a date with a guy you likely only vaguely remember . . ."

"Uh huh . . ."

"And *this* situation got off the bus . . ."

"What situation? Your situation? You mean the hair and the T-shirt and jeans?"

"And the face."

"What's wrong with your face?"

"No, I don't mean anything is explicitly wrong with me. I just mean . . . the whole package. This whole *thing* I've got going on is what walks off the bus to meet you for your date. How would you feel?"

"I, personally, would be intrigued and excited. I'd want to talk to you about your hair, because, face it, it's a bit of a conversation piece. And the rest of your 'situation' is . . . not something most male-attracted people would be disappointed by. But I can't speak for Katie. I don't know her. Maybe she can only get it up for redheads. Or she only likes guys who wear suits or something, I don't know, people are complicated. But I can say that if she's willing to go on this blind date, she's likely open to the possibility of liking *you*, however you are."

"—Whoa! Careful!"

"Oh, my gosh!"

"Are you all right, Gwen?"

"I guess we had to brake really fast for something? Yeah. I'm all right. I think I'm siding with your mother on the seat-belt issue, though. Are you all right?"

"Yeah, I'm okay. Shirley, you all right?"

"I spilled my damn chocolate milk,
but other than that I'm all right."

"Wow, Sam, look at how far everyone's luggage shifted in the overhead compartments."

"Jeez. I hope everyone's all right. I'm going to check it out real quick and make sure no one needs help. I'll be right back."

"Good, I'm glad he's gone for a minute."

"What's up, Shirley?"

"He doesn't recognize me because he keeps to himself on these trips for the most part, but I've taken many a bus ride with that boy over the years."

"Really?"

"Let me tell you. He's what they call a filial son. I've seen his mother before. Sometimes she comes to the bus station with him."

"Oh yeah?"

"Mmhmm. And she's not quite as big a piece of work as you might think, based on those phone calls, but I personally don't think she knows what she's got on her hands with that boy. Not every son is driving up the eastern seaboard to see their mamas once a month. I'm lucky if I see my son at Christmas. Of course, he lives in Las Vegas and it's more than just a little jaunt on the bus."

"I'm sorry to hear that."

"That's not the point. The point is, that boy is polite as can be. I've seen him haul luggage for folks, offer up his seat so families can sit together, share food, you name it. But I've never seen him out and out socialize."

"Really? He's so easy to talk to. Usually I'm the one asking all the questions. But he had me chatting about myself immediately, and I really never do that."

"Well, you must have the special sauce, hon. To bring it out of him. Or there's something going on with him, because I've certainly never seen him with blue hair before. So, just know that you're catching our boy at a very interesting time."

"He's headed back this way."

"Do with that what you will."

"Thanks, Shirley. Everything all right up there, Sam?"

"There was one very irritated teenager who'd spilled an entire bucket of fried chicken, but besides that, everyone was fine. The bus driver said there was a truck tire in the road."

"Wow."

"Oh, *no.*"

"What? What?!"

"Gwen. *Look.*"

"What!? Oh. I hadn't even noticed."

"You hadn't noticed that my *entire* tuna-fish sandwich had smashed against your pants?"

"I mean everything shifted around so suddenly! Shoot. Well . . ."

"Here. I usually keep a plastic bag . . . got it. We'll just wrap it up. Do . . . do you think your pants will be all right?"

"Let me see if I can do some damage control in the bathroom."

"Sure. Sure."

"Be right back."

"Good luck."

Chapter Two

Sam

Note to self: when you're lucky enough to sit next to a very attractive woman on a long bus ride, maybe don't bring up your mother so much. And probably don't give an extremely detailed overview of why you're a bad date. Or talk about a very embarrassing failed crush from your childhood. Oh, and definitely don't squash a tuna-fish sandwich on her pants.

This is why I normally don't talk to strangers.

Stranger danger is real, but it's me—I'm the danger. To myself.

You'd think after a decade of bus rides once a month I would be better at the whole seatmate bonding thing. But my typical MO is *find seat, say hello, put on headphones, vibe for five-ish hours, keep elbows from bumping seatmate, get off bus.*

But everything went screwy today. Starting with the peanut butter sandwich.

My mother hates smooth peanut butter with a passion. But her eyesight is bad if she doesn't wear her glasses and, you guessed it, she hates wearing her glasses. So she made a sandwich this morning with accidentally purchased smooth peanut butter and didn't realize her mistake until she had a mouthful. Which also means that when I should have been catching a ride with a neighbor to the bus station, instead I was missing that ride and sprinting to the grocery store to buy her the chunky peanut butter. And then catching the T to a bus to another bus to catch, well, *this* bus. Which means I am now the collective bus bathroom chaperone.

Would I trade the worst seat on the bus for a better seat?

I would not.

Because the worst seat on the bus comes with, by far, the best seatmate on the bus.

I've sat next to cute girls on the bus before. It would be weird if I hadn't, considering I've taken this exact bus ride over a hundred times. But the thing is, when you initiate conversation with a stranger on a bus ride, this phenomenon usually happens to their eyes. Just for a moment, panic flares up like a wildfire and consumes their soul. When it flames out, there is a sort of dead resignation there. They've surrendered themselves to the reality that they are, in fact, sitting next to someone who talks to strangers on bus rides. Then their fingers start to inch toward their headphones or their book and they smile and nod, while inside they desperately, frantically search for a way, *any* way out of this forced hell of a conversation, no matter how polite it might be.

I have gone out of my way to never inflict that on another soul.

Especially not on the cute girls who have to endure crap like that from dudes all the time. I would much rather they think I'm uninterested than have them worry about getting hit on for five hours straight while they're trapped in an enclosed space with me.

But Gwen talked to me first. And I did not see panic firebomb her soul. And . . . I wouldn't actually call her cute? She's more . . . *interesting* than cute. Straight, dark hair parted down the middle, pale skin, sly brown eyes, a big nose, and a very white smile with two overlapping teeth on the bottom. She's the kind of pretty that probably didn't perform so well in middle school but performs very well on a long bus ride in adulthood.

I'm doing my very best not to turn my immediate attraction to her into a . . . thing—

"Hey, Sam?"

"Yeah?"

"These pants are a lost cause for now. Hand me that backpack? I've gotta change."

"Oh. Sure."

"Thanks!"

My fingers are still tingling from where they just touched hers when I passed the bag to her. My phone buzzes in my pocket and I grimace. I know without looking that it's my mother who has just texted me. It's pretty much always my mother.

Mama's boy? you ask.

Usually it's not this bad.

This just so happened to be one of the worst weekends of my mother's life. So, there I was, sprinting to buy peanut butter, and now I'm allowing myself to be badgered into likely bad dates with near strangers. Once she's feeling a little better she'll go back to calling me the much-more-manageable once a day and I'll be in less danger of grinding my teeth down to flat little Stegosaurus nubs.

But for now, I read her text asking me if I brought anything I can change into on the bus or if I'll be wearing the same jeans and T-shirt to my date.

Shockingly, I text back, *I didn't bring any date-night clothes for this bus ride. Yes, I'll be in the T-shirt and jeans. Which is yet another reason why you should call her and tell her not to meet me at the bus stop!*

She says nothing in return, which is tactical on her part.

I cannot believe that she somehow managed to get me a date with Katie McConnick. It's just so . . . random. Yes, Katie was a very big former crush. But I haven't thought about her in years. I definitely didn't carry that flame for very long after we both moved away. And the thought of walking off a bus in a few hours and trying to clock her reaction to me and trying to clock my own reaction to her . . .

I should probably be excited, right?

A second chance to get all those old feelings off my chest? That's what Gwen was saying anyhow.

But I'm really not excited.

In fact, the thought of the bus stop is making me feel a kind of . . . restless uneasiness. Usually, the bus stop is the only thing I wanna see right about now. But today . . .?

My mother texts again and I'm sighing and shaking my head down at my phone when Gwen comes out of the bathroom, freshly changed.

Chapter Three

"Wow. That's quite the outfit, Gwen."

"I know. It's the only other thing I had to wear, besides pajamas. And my pajamas were not designed for public consumption."

"So, you must have had some sort of fancy shindig this weekend? If you brought that to wear."

"Yup. You are officially being treated to Gwen Cellar's formal-wear outfit. Do you wanna just scoot in? I can sit on the aisle."

"Gwen, I absolutely refuse to subject you to the bathroom seat. You can slide in. Here . . . So . . . it's a . . . girl tux?"

"Yeah. I wear it when I want to feel like James Bond. Or when nice men smash tuna-fish sandwiches across my bus pants."

"I'm really sorry about that, by the way."

"I was thinking, at least it wasn't something that might permanently stain. Could have been a meatball sub."

"No, if it had been a meatball sub I'd have eaten it about fifty miles back. Your pants would have never paid the price."

"Ah, fate. What a cruel mistress."

"Seriously, though. You look really . . . excellent in that outfit. I've never worn a tux before but I don't think I'd pull it off like that."

"If it's a good tux, anybody can pull it off. That's the secret to menswear. If it's tailored well it looks good on anyone. Even women. I've never been much of a dresses person. I think they look nice on other people, but whenever I wear one, no matter what style it is, I always get this awful, itchy, housewifey feeling."

"Ah. And you didn't want to feel like a housewife this weekend. You wanted to feel like James Bond."

"Yeah."

"Just for the thrill of feeling like James Bond? Or . . . you needed some kind of armor? A costume?"

"You . . . Why do I want to tell you stuff?"

"Huh?"

"You're like Dory or something. With your big eyes and your blue hair. And I never talk about this stuff but you're making it seem very easy right now."

"Well, it kind of makes sense. I don't have short-term memory loss like Dory. But there aren't generally a lot of consequences to talking about personal stuff with a random person you'll likely never see again, you know? Your secrets are safe with me."

"Well, I sit next to a lot of strangers on a lot of different modes of transportation and I never tell them anything."

"Well, if it's any consolation I've had a lot of busmates and I've never asked any of them about their clothes. And for the record, you haven't actually told me anything yet. Is it armor? A costume?"

"Both, I guess? Family engagements are always like that for me. I need a liiiiittle bit of fortification."

"Was it your whole family?"

"Every single member on my father's side. Thirty or so of us."

"Wow. Big family! On my mom's side, it's only me, my mom, Aunt Laura and my cousin Mike."

"And your dad's side?"

"There's actually nobody left on my dad's side. His parents have been gone for decades. He passed away when I was a kid and his brother passed away a few years ago."

"Oh, Sam. I'm so sorry."

"Thanks. It's okay, though. It was a long time ago."

"Is that part of why you and your mom are so close?"

"Definitely. She calls me the ace up her sleeve. It's been that way since I was eight. And she was always the ace up my sleeve, too. Especially during my teenage years. But as you grow up, you kind of become your own ace, you know? And I think as I've needed her less and less she's started to need me more and more. And now . . . here we are. Peanut-butter runs and bathroom seats."

"Huh?"

"Oh, I'm usually early for the bus so I can get a seat at the front. But today I did an unexpected peanut-butter run for my mom and ended up being late."

"Ah. I see. That's how you ended up back here with the rest of the truants."

"Why were you late?"

"I actually made incredible time. I asked my cab driver to get me to south station as fast as humanly possible and he really rose to the occasion. I mean, I had to cover my eyes the entire ride and we almost drove off a bridge at one point, but he really earned his tip. I got here so late just because I only realized I needed to get back to New York at the last second. I'm lucky there was still a ticket left. I think I probably bought the last one."

"Yeah, it's usually not quite so full. I wonder what the deal is today."

"So, you know this route pretty well?"

"I am here a lot. Let's just say that."

"What's that expression on your face?"

"I'm just trying not to think about that old adage, *you are what you do.*"

"Because by that math . . ."

"I am a discount bus ride and I'm not sure I want to admit that."

"You are what you do, huh? There must be other things you do that could tell you who you are, no?"

"Mmmm, maybe. But I don't want to compare with you. Considering you're a world-traveling photographer and writer. I think your *do*s are more interesting than mine."

"Come on . . . what else do you do besides ride the bus?"

"I see friends, read mystery novels, watch TV. Oh! Okay, this is cool, I long-distance run."

"That's very cool! When you say long distance you mean, like marathons?"

"Yeah. I've run two marathons and one ultra-marathon. And I'd like to do another."

"What's an ultra-marathon?"

"I think technically anything that's longer than a marathon, but the one I did was fifty miles."

"*Fifty miles?!*"

"Haha. You look disgusted."

"No! I'm not disgusted I'm just . . . is that really humanly possible? You ran fifty miles *at once*?"

"I mean, it took me all day."

"Well, I should hope so! Fifty miles? You've gotta be kidding me. And you said that you want to do another one?"

"I'd be honest and tell you that I'd like to do a hundred-miler but I'm scared of your reaction."

"Don't say a hundred miles! I can't even think about that! Your poor legs! Your knees! Oh, my God, why would you do that to yourself?"

"I know, a lot of it is really . . . grueling. But that's kind of the best part? It's hard to explain. I think . . . running that far, and training for it, makes everything else easier in comparison. It's kind of like, well, if I can do *that*, then I can definitely do *this*—you know?"

"So, when you increase your endurance for those races, you kind of increase your endurance for everything in life?"

"At least that's the way it's worked for me."

"Do you get spectators at these races?"

"At the finish lines, yeah. But it's not quite as . . . triumphant as you might think. Nobody looks good at the end of a fifty-mile race."

"Well, I'd like to see it. If you do the hundred-miler, I'm definitely showing up at the finish line with a cheeseburger and a milkshake."

"For me?"

"I figure you'll need the calories."

"I will definitely puke if you try to feed me a cheeseburger and a milkshake at the end of a hundred-mile race."

"See? That's how much I know about real exercising."

"You don't exercise?"

"I run. But, like, three miles at a time, as fast as I can, once or twice a week. I really just try to get it over with."

"Ah, I see, so you get all the pain and discomfort and none of the runner's high."

"Everybody talks about a runner's high, but I'd swear it's a myth."

"Three miles as fast as you can . . . Speaking of poor knees, yours must be a mess!"

"Doesn't everyone have bad knees? Isn't that just the way the world works?"

"You are what you do."

"And I've got the knees to prove it."

". . . Sorry."

"You've got the yawns. Sleepy?"

"A little. I never sleep well at my mom's house. I always get tired at this point of the drive. Something about how the highway is here. It's kind of . . . soothing?"

"Yeah, we're actually cruising along now. Do you want to get some shut-eye?"

"Well, maybe just a catnap."

"Sure. See you when you wake up!"

Chapter Four

Gwen

This man has a very heavy head. I know because its entire weight is currently resting on my shoulder, which means I'm smooshed up against the window. I kind of don't mind because Sam is, so far, a very nice man and it's been a long time since a very nice man has smooshed me up against anything.

Tuna-fish sandwich pants aside, I've had a string of very good luck recently. An incredible work opportunity, a crappy roommate who spontaneously decided to move in with her girlfriend so I didn't even have to go through the awkward pain of asking her to move out, and now, this: A handsome blue-haired man who laughs shyly, doesn't manspread, and genuinely seems to enjoy chatting with me.

He's my good luck charm, I've just decided. Not that he's an object. He's a living, breathing person with personhood and free will and all that. So, instead of a charm, let's just say he's my good luck man.

And today I need a good luck man because in just a few hours I'll be sitting across a table from someone I've been wanting to meet for years and she will hopefully, *hopefully* be providing my career with the turbo boost I didn't even know it needed.

Here's the thing about being someone with a job like mine. Sometimes you can't even quite envision what the future might look like. Some jobs are like ladders. You know what's on the rung above you because, likely, there's someone already there, showing you exactly what that job might look like. That is not my job at all.

I have no idea where next year's paycheck will come from or how much it will be for. For the most part, I try to save where I can and enjoy myself in the meantime . . . but every once in a while I start waking up in the middle of the night in a cold sweat asking myself why the hell I didn't go to undergrad and study photography or journalism and am not on staff somewhere that offers health insurance and a five-year plan.

But then I remember that I've always been a hustler. I've always been able to be conservative in the lean times and make it through to the other side. If I'm patient and work hard, I create opportunities. I just have to trust myself to pull the rabbit out of the hat. So far, I've never come up empty.

And this meeting tonight is one hell of a rabbit. Meet a hero? Check. Secure a book deal? Double check. Ensure the next year's worth of income? Triple check.

Yes, please.

Sam shifts and sighs against my shoulder and even though I can't feel my fingertips anymore, I don't adjust him. He's only been asleep for ten minutes or so and I don't want to wake him yet. He really looked like he needed the sleep. I can see his phone lighting up through the fabric of his pants and I hope it's not vibrating and disturbing his sleep. He's going to need all his wits about him for his big date. Katie McConnick. I'd be lying if I said I wasn't a little bit jealous of her.

She gets to stand on the sidewalk, likely having just primped for a date, and watch this tall hunk of man unfold himself from the bus for her. I will be trailing behind in last night's wrinkled formal wear waving goodbye to Sam for ever and sprinting across the city to get to work.

I bet she was a pretty girl in high school.

I was *not* a pretty girl in high school. I had my charms, i.e. boobs and a bad attitude (a certain type of high-school boy was very attracted to that particular combination). But I was mostly an outcast and high school is something I somewhat fondly look back on as more of a gauntlet I survived than anything else.

But Katie McConnick sounds like a peach. Perfectly crush-worthy. Someone Sam's mother is so excited for him to fall in love with that she's already called him multiple times about it on this one bus ride.

His phone is still lighting up in his pocket.

If I had to wager a guess, I'd say it's probably his mom blowing him up right now.

A filial son, Shirley had said. Carefully, so I don't disturb him, I take out my phone and look up the definition of "filial".

Of or due from a son or daughter, the dictionary tells me.

Hmmm.

I was worried it was something like that. Not because of what it means about Sam. It's nice that he's a filial son. I just hate learning a word like that because . . . I am certainly not a filial daughter.

"Due" from a daughter. What exactly *is* due from a daughter? And why?

Out of a poke-the-paper-cut sort of curiosity I open my own texting app and scroll through the conversations, trying to find the last time either of my parents texted me. Scroll, scroll, scroll. When I've gone back four months in time and still haven't seen anything from either of them, I sigh and black my phone and slip it away. True, they're more voicemail people than text message people, and to be fair, if I had texted *them* in the last four months, even to no response, those text chains would be higher in the queue.

Sam's head nods forward and I use my index finger against his forehead to balance him back against my shoulder. All I can see from this vantage point is a cloud of spiky indigo. He smells like mint shampoo. I hope he isn't using anything too abrasive to wash his hair or that color won't last more than a week. Although he'll look nice when it starts to fade. Indigo Sam will be Blueberry Sam will be Periwinkle Sam and then Sky Blue Sam and then, eventually, he'll be a washed-out Easter egg and he'll have to decide what the heck to do with the skunk stripe down the middle of his dark brown head.

The bus cruises under a tunnel and in the sudden dark my reflection smiles back at me. The white of my teeth is unexpected enough my smile drops away. I peer back at the heavy blue weight on my shoulder. He's making me smile to myself without realizing it. What kind of magic is this?

Seriously though, why am I talking about my life to this man? Is he right? That we'll probably never see each other again so why not unload some dirty details and move on? Is it Niles Shaw texting me increasingly annoying jabs? Is it the impending meeting looming over me? Is it my parents frowning over the table last night? All of it is just too much at once and I have to unload to a stranger? Or is it that, no matter the circumstance, when you meet a soft, smiley, fluffy blue cloud, you just lie down and get comfortable?

Is my life this stressful or is Sam just this lovely?

I fiddle with the cuff of my jacket and frown at the speck of red wine that left a kidney-bean shaped stain near the button. It seems apt that a night like last night would have left a stain on my favorite formal outfit. What a load of baloney that whole event was.

I'm not a cynic, especially not about love. I've interviewed hundreds of people over the course of my career and most of them have something good to say about how love has changed their lives for the better. You try listening to an eighty-eight-year-old man explain why he still wears his deceased wife's engagement ring on a chain around his neck and then tell me love isn't real. It's real, people.

It was just not exactly present in the event space at the Boston Marriott last night. Every single member of my dad's family present and accounted for, all taking turns to look at me like I'm an alien posing as a human.

I get together with them, family-reunion-style, and the whole high-school outcast thing comes back full force.

Sam's feet start to wake up, rolling at the ankle and then pointing at the toe. Each foot is roughly the length of a loaf of bread. Now that I really look, his knees are practically jammed against the seat in front of him. He barely fits in that seat. His hands wake up next. They open like starfish and then flop onto his knees. I know the exact second his brain comes back online because he suddenly sits up, ramrod straight, and looks at me with pure mortification.

Chapter Five

"I fell asleep on you."

"Sure did."

"Oh, my God, look at how crammed up against the window you are. I'm so sorry! I must have been so much dead weight."

"I'd tell you that it's totally fine, but I don't think you're gonna believe me."

"How could it be fine?! Look, I wrinkled the sleeve of your tux."

"You seem pretty determined to beat yourself up so I'll just relax over here in the meantime. Tell me when it's over."

"You're seriously not put out at all? I'm like, ten times bigger than you are."

"Besides tingly fingers, there was no collateral damage. I swear."

"Your hand fell asleep? Here. I know this trick. You have to make a hand sandwich."

"Huh?"

"You flatten your hand between two other things and make your hand like the lettuce in a sandwich and when you apply even pressure, the tingling stops for the most part."

"Okay, like this?"

"Not exactly. Um. Honestly, it works best if someone else does it for you."

"Oh. By all means."

"Um, sure. So, I'll just use my hands, okay?"

"Yup. Hurry, the pins and needles are crescendoing!"

"Okay. So. Here. Is that better?"

"Aw. It really is a hand sandwich. Dang, you have big hands. I can't even *see* my hand in there."

"Um. Yeah . . . Okay, I'm gonna loosen pressure now."

"Sure . . . Wait! No! Too many pins and needles. Just keep sandwiching for another minute."

"All right."

"I think you got a bunch of texts while you were sleeping."

"Yeah. I'm sure I did. I'll check them later."

"When you're not hand sandwiching?"

"Exactly. So . . . should we play a road-trip game?"

"I'm thinking of a number between one and a thousand. Go."

"Hahaha. I'll take that as a no, you don't want to play a road-trip game. Fair enough, I've killed a lot of time on this bus ride before, but I've never done it with games."

"You're a podcast guy?"

"Usually music. Occasionally a book on tape."

"I believe we call those audio books now."

"Ah. Right."

"Books on tape were what you checked out from the library when you had to endure thirty hours in the back seat next to your sister on a drive to Albuquerque."

"That . . . sounds . . . literal?"

"Yup. Once a year my family made that drive to see my grandparents. The only thing that kept me alive was my Walkman. You should've seen how many just-in-case batteries I'd pack."

"You checked out books on tape from the library? Remember those gigantic plastic shell cases they'd come in?"

"Vividly."

"What kinds of books were you into?"

"Well, for visual reading, I was into everything. Fantasy, mystery, romance, you name it. But for those long car rides? It was Stephen King all the way."

"Ah. A horror fan?"

"Sort of. I love horror in the moment, and then hate it for about five weeks after when I have to pee in the middle of the night and can't make myself pull the blankets off my head."

"Honey, you move quick! You're already holding hands?"

"Oh! No! I was just helping with a, um, medical issue. Sorry, Gwen. I forgot I was still sandwiching . . . Anyhow. How's the hand?"

"It's all good now. How you doing, Shirley?"

"I remembered the peanut brittle I packed. Here, you kids have some."

"Thanks, Shirley!"

"Thank you, Shirley!"

"I'm gonna sleep now. With my mask and earphones in, so wake me up when the bus gets to NYC, you hear?"

"Yes, ma'am. Sleep well . . . Hrmrmph!"

"Sam, was that ominous crack your *tooth*?"

"Do not, I repeat, do NOT eat this peanut brittle."

"Did you just lose a crown?"

"Close call, but no. Seriously though, do not eat this."

"What should we do with it? She's gonna notice if we don't . . . Wow. You're not gonna . . . Yup. Yup, that's exactly what you're doing. Okay. That was very quick thinking. Straight down the bus toilet."

"No one should have to endure what my mouth just endured."

"Hey."

"Yeah?"

"Manspread a little."

"Huh?"

"You can manspread into my space."

"Um."

"Seriously."

"I've been firmly instructed that's a big ixnay."

"I'm telling you that in this particular instance, it's not. I can't stand looking at your poor knees anymore."

"What's wrong with my knees?"

"They look like they're slowly losing the will to live in captivity. You've got Free Willy knees."

"Free Willy definitely didn't have knees. He was a whale."

"Just spread out into my space, okay? I've got plenty of available real estate over here. I paid sixteen whole dollars for it and I can use it however I want. I'm gifting it to you."

"If you're sure . . . You can tell me to beat it whenever . . . *Wow.*"

"Better?"

"Roughly one million times better. I'm going to try not to get used to this. Odds are the next seatmate I have won't be so pro-manspreading."

"I'm not either, usually. But you've already fallen asleep on me and held my hand, so what's a little knee-action between bus friends?"

"I'm usually a very unobtrusive seatmate, I swear."

"Shirley says you keep to yourself, but when people need help you're very obliging."

"Oh. She's seen me before?"

"She said that she's ridden the bus with you a ton of times but that you didn't know because you mind your own business for the most part. Unless you're helping little old ladies get their umbrellas open and whatnot."

"She didn't actually say the umbrella part, did she? Because that part is definitely an exaggeration."

"I added the umbrella part. She just said that you help people with their luggage a lot."

"Well."

"I take it from your blush that it's true?"

"Anyways. I can't believe I didn't recognize Shirley if I've taken the bus with her before. Maybe I'm horribly unobservant."

"Maybe you've had other things on your mind."

"For an entire decade? I think that might be just a little too much benefit of the doubt. I'm not that deep."

"Hey, Sam?"

"Yeah?"

"Does that luggage look like it's sliding out of the overhead to you?"

"Hm? Where? Oh, shit. Watch out, kid!"

"Oh, damn! That was close."

"Don't worry. I got it. Are you all right? Is everybody all right?"

"Yeah, man—thank you so much!"

"No problem. I think this might be safer at your feet."

"Yeah. It almost killed me. Thanks, man."

"Sure. Well, I'll get back to my seat."

"Well, *that* was exciting."

"Are you all right, Gwen? You look . . . something?"

"I . . . can't believe you made that catch. You were so far away. You have very long arms, Sam."

"Oh. Yes. I do. Lanky. I was on the basketball team in high school. Are you sure you're all right?"

"Yes, I'm fine. That was just cool is all. You were like a superhero."

"Oh, my God. All I did was catch a suitcase."

"From like ten feet away! If there had been music in the background it could have been an action scene."

"Why are you blushing? You're making *me* blush now. Let's talk about something else. Something other than my long arms."

"Okay, ummm, topic, topic, what's a good topic?"

"See? Topics are weirdly hard to think of when you need one!"

"Yeah, I guess so, huh? I mean, what do people normally talk about instead of arm length? Foot size? No! That's weird. How about . . ."

"Hobbies? Favorite restaurant in NYC? Occupation?"

"Boom. Boom. Boom. Sam, you're cured! You're a topic wizard."

"Did any of them strike your fancy?"

"Oh. Yeah. What'd you say your work was?"

"Oh. Okay, yeah. I'm a physical therapist."

"Oh. Wow!"

"You sound surprised."

"I think I was expecting more of an office job? Because you said they might not let you keep your hair dyed."

"Maybe they will. But none of my colleagues have brightly dyed hair and I've never checked the employee manual about it."

"So, how'd you get into that line of work?"

"Well . . . it's always been a job I thought was cool. When I was a kid my dad had to get a huge chunk of the muscles in his leg surgically removed. Cancer."

"Oh, my gosh."

"Yeah. It was really rough and whenever he'd come home from the hospital, or from an appointment, he always seemed so . . . dispirited. But he had this PT named Doreen who was a total hardass softie."

"Hardass softie? Is that a thing?"

"Yeah. She just . . . knew when to push and when to be sweet. Anyhow, she'd come to our house to work with Dad and whenever their sessions were over he always seemed tired, but . . . determined. And I just liked seeing what she did for him. She really helped him. Gave him hope. And I wanted to do that for people. So. Yeah. Twenty-odd years later, here I am."

"So, you really like your work?"

"I do . . ."

"But? I think I heard a 'but' in there."

"You probably never feel this way because of the nature of your job, but . . . well, my dad was an electrician. He started training to be an electrician at eighteen. He was fully employed on his own by twenty-one and he worked until he was forced into retirement because of his illness. He never missed a day of work, barely took vacations, and never considered a career change. My mom is the same. She went to school to become a teacher, became one, and taught in the public school system for forty-two years until she retired. Badda bing badda boom."

"And now you're seeing the next few decades span out before you and even though you love your job you feel so claustrophobic you want to scream?"

"Wow."

"I'm wrong?"

"No, you're exactly right. More or less. God, I feel so guilty even saying it. I mean . . . I'm so lucky to be gainfully employed. And I like my co-workers, my clients, my workplace, but I've already been working, five days a week for almost a decade, working and paying off student loan debt, and . . . I guess I just feel a little hamster-wheelish sometimes."

"Could you take a sabbatical?"

"Not and keep my job. But . . . I've considered applying for a new job, elsewhere, and requesting that the start time is a few months down the road so that I'd have a little time to . . . reboot in between."

"That's a great idea! What would you do with that time if it all worked out?"

"Travel, I think."

"Obviously my favorite thing ever. Where would you want to go?"

"I'm not sure. Like I said, I've never been anywhere."

"Go to Portugal! You can eat sardines by the sea. They're big on sardines over there."

"Oh. Um. I have some money saved but I don't know about blowing it all on a European vacation."

"There are ways to travel cheaply. I mean . . . you take the Megabus once a month, so I'm guessing you're not dead-set on luxury. You could stay in hostels, buy your food from grocery stores, you could do work/stay shares and get free room and board. Or, what about medical missions of some kind? Do physical therapists ever volunteer their time in that way?"

"Definitely. But I think I might be looking for more of a *break* break."

"Sure. Of course. After a decade of straight work, it sounds like you really deserve one. Oh, this is so fun! I love planning travel for other people."

"Don't get too excited. Full disclosure, I've been considering something like this for years but I've never done anything about it."

"Maybe you should start small."

"What do you mean?"

"Do you have any vacation days coming your way?"

"I have three coming my way this quarter."

"Can you decide when you use them?"

"Yeah, actually, it rotates who gets to request for dates first and this quarter I get to request first. Which means I'll almost definitely get the dates I want."

"Okay, so maybe plan a small vacation for yourself. Somewhere you've always wanted to go. And then search for cheap tickets and see if you could swing it."

"Okayyyyy, well, I don't have a passport, so it would have to be stateside . . . I've always wanted to go to New Orleans."

"*Excellent* choice. Ooh! There's a New Orleans culinary festival coming up in about a month and a half. All these restaurants and chefs participate. But there's also street food and people selling home cooking from their doorsteps. I've never gone but people say it's absolutely amazing. The best food you'll ever eat."

"Oh. That . . . actually sounds exactly like something I'd be into. Hold on, let me search the dates. Oh! It's over a long weekend. So, I'd get that day off as a freebie."

"Which means with that extra day you could fly a Wednesday to a Tuesday which would probably make the flights cheaper."

"Okay, let me check that . . . Whoa."

"What is it?"

"These are . . . *not* expensive flights. I mean, the layovers are absurdly long, but . . . I could afford this."

"Mmmmmmm."

"What?"

"I'm just reveling in the bright sunshine of someone else's travel enthusiasm. Oh, no. You put your phone away."

"Well, I hate to take away the sunshine. And it's a really nice idea. I might do it. Really. But I have to talk to my work and secure the dates first. And then I'll need to make sure I can afford a place to stay."

"That makes sense. Oh, your phone is buzzing again."

"Yeah, I . . . oh! It's not from my mom."

"Really?"

"You don't have to sound *so* shocked. I have friends. Oh. Shoot."

"Bad news?"

"My friend Paloma is getting evicted from her apartment because the landlord sold it to a developer and she's having a hell of a time finding a place to live. She was going to move into our friend Vera's apartment, because Vera is moving in with her boyfriend, but then Vera just got notified that her rent is going up, so now Paloma can't afford that place either."

"Ugh. I've been there. Finding a place to live in NYC can be soul-killing. Terrifying. You name it."

"I wish my apartment were big enough to help her out but I'm in a studio. It would just be awkward."

"Oh. So . . . Paloma's not a romantic interest?"

"Loma?! No. I mean, she's great. But we have more of a family relationship than anything else. Besides, she dates short, fashionable men."

"Short and fashionable men. That's a type all right."

"She doesn't like it when she feels like someone is looming over her. Or crowding her."

"I take it she's the one who informed you of the evils of manspreading?"

"One of the many. She's a very instructive friend."

"So, you're obviously not short. But you're not *not* fashionable."

"Thanks?"

"I mean, I wouldn't say that you're definitely *un*fashionable."

"Again—thanks?"

"I'll just shut up now. Sorry. Where's the peanut brittle when you need it?"

"I think what you were saying was a compliment? I'll just take it as a compliment."

"Good. Yes. Okay. So . . . you have Paloma, who you don't date, and Vera, who I'm assuming you also don't date . . ."

"Yeah. I met Paloma first. We both took a manage-your-finances class at the 92nd Street Y and we hit it off. Vera's her best friend, so I kind of got absorbed into their friendship a bit. I don't get to see them as often as I'd like though; they're both pretty busy, I'm gone at least one weekend a month, and we live in different boroughs."

"They sound really great."

"Are most of your friends in the city? Or all over the world?"

"Does it feel like we're slowing down?"

"Yeah, I think we might be hitting some traffic."

"Shoot. Uh . . . what was the question? My friends? Oh, I have some friends in the city, and some people I really like. But yes, most of my closest people are all abroad."

"Do you stay in touch with them?"

"Some of them I stay in really good touch. Email and group chats and whatnot. Some of them I don't stay in touch with at all but when I'm in their city they make time for me and it's like I never left . . . What's that look for?"

"Oh, nothing. It's just that I was realizing how different you and I are. I really need, like, a core group of people to depend on. And it sounds like you're comfortable letting people in and out of your life more freely."

"Comfortable? Yeah. I guess. I mean, that's just the way my life works, so . . ."

"Right."

"Wow, now we're *really* slowing down. Can you see out the front window? How long the traffic goes for? Please let it just be a little slow-down that we're about to skirt around and then be past."

"I can't see much from back here, but I can tell you that this is always the trafficky part on the way back down to New York. The construction gets down to two lanes for a couple miles and everyone bottlenecks."

"Oh, God."

"Are you all right?"

"Fine. Fine. When you've done this before, how long does it usually take?"

"The entire ride? I mean . . . I've done it early, *early* on a Sunday morning in as little as four hours. But on a Sunday afternoon? With construction and accidents and stuff? It's taken up to seven hours before."

"Seven?!? That would put us home at . . . *eight thirty*? Oh, I'm so screwed."

"Seven hours is a worst-case scenario. Right now, this is just still run-of-the-mill traffic. I wouldn't worry about it just yet."

"I knew I should have just coughed up for the plane ticket. But last minute it was so expensive and I was already eating tomorrow's train ticket and . . . oh, I'm so *screwed*."

"A plane? Between Boston and New York? I never understood why people do that. Once you get out to Logan and then home from whichever NY airport you fly into, the whole experience takes just as long as the train."

"I know, that was my logic too. But all the train tickets were already sold out so I had no choice but to take the bus and I thought I caught it early enough, but I didn't think there would be *seven hours* of traffic."

"So far there's only been, like, a few minutes of traffic."

"Right. Right. Let's not panic yet."

". . ."

". . ."

"Can I ask . . . what exactly are you panicking about?"

"I'm not panicking yet, remember?"

"Oh, of course. You're very calm. Do you need another hand sandwich? I think you're going to burn a hole through your tux if you keep tapping at that rate."

"Okay, so maybe I'm panicking a little."

"And what are you panicking a little about?"

"Does the name Florine Weatherbell mean anything to you?"

"Other than being one of the coolest names I've ever heard before . . . no."

"Well, she's this kind of infamous Manhattan socialite. She was the toast of the town in like . . . the fifties and sixties. She used to be a photographer and she had an invite to every *it* party there ever was. She was friends with all the big names. And I mean the *big* names. Warhol, Yves St. Laurent, Judy Chicago, she was friends with Jackie Onassis, later on, Basquiat. She's donated a lot of photos she's taken and sometimes they'll display them at the library and seriously, the woman knew *everyone*. But sometime in the early nineties she stopped going out, and stopped socializing and became kind of this famed recluse. Anyhow, in addition to being a photographer and socialite-slash-recluse, she's also a known collector. She has a huge collection of art and rare books, but . . . what I'm most interested in . . . is that she is rumored to have the most extensive, most expensive private collection of jewelry in New York City. Maybe even in the United States. Historical pieces, pieces from the fashion world, commissioned pieces, one-of-a-kind stones, you name it."

"Wow. She sounds like the one person in the world you'd most want to interview."

"Exactly. Except—"

"She's a famed recluse."

"*Exactly.* Apparently when you have one of the largest private collections of jewelry in the world, you're very picky about who can come into and out of your house."

"Go figure."

"So, here's the thing. About three months ago, an editor from a photography-based publishing house got in touch with me."

"Cool!"

"Yes. It was very exciting. She's apparently a huge fan of my blog and really wants to get my stuff published into a book."

"Gwen!"

"I know. A dream come true, right?"

"I mean . . . don't you want that?"

"I want it so bad I can barely see straight. But there's a couple of catches."

"Aren't there always?"

"Sure seems like it."

"What are they?"

"Well, number one—she's not in charge of acquisitions."

"Oh, brother."

"Yeah. And the guy who is, has said that he likes my stuff, but that books like these sell better when there is at least one 'person of extreme interest' marketed in them. He was hoping for a celeb of some kind. So, he was pitching all these movie stars and musicians and politicians that I could interview. Which . . . I would if it meant sealing the book deal. But I wasn't . . . I'm not . . . Celeste, my editor, could tell that interviewing someone just because they are famous and a good angle for my book wasn't very exciting to me. So, she asked me who I'd really want to interview and I just said it, 'Well, Florine Weatherbell is kind of my hero, but of course we'll never get an interview with her.' And then—"

"Are you about to tell me that Celeste is a magician?"

"Pretty much. Celeste pitched Florine to Mr. Acquisitions and he said well, sure, if you can get her. And so, for the last two months, Celeste has been trying literally everything she can to get an appointment with Florine."

"Holy smokes. And she got one?"

"Apparently, Celeste figured out that Florine's granddaughter, who is one of the only people who freely goes in and out the house, is a huge fan of this one K-pop group. So, she befriended her online, and actually got totally sucked into the K-pop group herself—I think they're going to a concert together later this summer. Anyhow, she got the granddaughter to look at my work and ask Florine if she'd have any interest in meeting with me. And then *bam*. Celeste called me at the crack of dawn this morning and said, come back from Boston a day early because, honey, I got you the interview. It's today at seven p.m. on the Upper East Side."

"WOW."

"Yeah. But I'm stuck on this bus in traffic."

"Crap."

"Yeah."

"Okay. So . . . the bus left at noon."

"And I figured an extra hour of traffic. So, I thought we'd be there around five. Which would still give me two hours to get up to her house."

"That's reasonable. Super reasonable. Look, before we start to panic over this let's just check the traffic. Here. Look! That's not nearly as much red as there sometimes is. We might not get you home at five on the dot, but I think you're gonna make it. Honestly, from the bus drop-off point, even if we got in at six fifteen, you'd still be able to make it to her house on time."

"Okay. Okay . . . I love that you said before 'we' start to panic."

"Well, I mean, it's probably not productive if we both panic, but yeah, if sitting in traffic means missing out on the opportunity of a lifetime, I think the panic starts to become contagious."

"But you said there's not too much red."

"Not too much at all. We'll be cruising again in . . . I'm

gonna guess twenty minutes. And then the miles will just tick past."

"Are you ready for the other catch?"

"Oh, no, I forgot there was another catch."

"Yeah. Getting there exactly on time *might* work. But getting there as early as possible is better because . . . here, let me show you . . . remember I mentioned I have a rival? His name is Niles Shaw. And this is his work."

"Um."

"Are you noticing that his photos and interviews are pretty much exactly the same as mine?"

"I mean, yours are better, but . . ."

"Well, scroll back through his feed. You'll notice that he used to be a landscape photographer and then right around the time my work started to get some internet traction, he abruptly shifted focus."

"He's copying you?"

"Blatantly. He even hops around to the same cities as me, trying to get the jump on my vibe. He's a total and complete scavenger and completely unrepentant about it."

"How come he gets away with it?"

"Well, he's got, like, ten times the followers that I do and a lot of them are very loyal to him. Even the fact that I coined my style first doesn't sway them, they still think that I'm the one copying him. And I never want to encourage animosity online, or fan wars, so I don't feed into any of the online discussions about it."

"Doesn't it make you want to scream into a pillow, though?"

"Constantly. And look, this is what he looks like. Don't you just want to . . . shove a pie in his face or something?"

"Yes. Absolutely. Of *course* he's movie-star handsome. And look at that smile. The world is his oyster. He definitely deserves pie face."

"So, anyhow, Celeste let me know, through the granddaughter, that when Florine Weatherbell was checking out my work online she also saw Shaw's work and said, well, why don't you invite him too?"

"Noooooooooooo. He's going to be there?"

"Yup. But get this, she's eccentric and brilliant and can have anything she wants, so she said, whichever of them gets here first can have the interview."

"NOOOOOOOOOOOO."

"I know."

"Do you think there's a chance that he's staking out there?"

"Well, he's based in LA and I was looking at his socials earlier and he posted something from LAX. So, he's definitely flying in for it. So I don't think he'll beat me by miles. But he definitely might get there first."

"Which was why you thought the bus would be a safe bet."

"I didn't count on seven hours of traffic, but yeah, I saw his post, did the math on timing and figured that I could still beat him to her house."

"Okay. Well. I get that. And look, there's nothing that we can do from the bathroom seats of this bus, right?"

"Right."

"So, in the meantime, should we talk about something else to get your mind off of it?"

"Great idea."

"So . . . is that your camera? It's way bigger than I'd imagined."

"This? Yes. This is my baby. No, that's not an apt description because honestly, this camera takes care of me as much as I take care of it. So, instead . . . let's call it my life partner."

"Can I see it?"

"Sure."

"Oh, wow. It's really beautiful. Full of character."

"Right?"

"Oh, but look, there's a little hole in the case."

"I know. A TSA agent was too rough a couple months ago. He felt bad, but I was late for my flight so I just gathered all my stuff and sprinted. I haven't gotten it fixed yet. It's mostly just a cosmetic tear."

"I can fix it."

"Hm?"

"Sure. Hold on. I've got . . . somewhere . . . yes! Here. I keep this in case of emergencies."

"You keep a sewing kit in case of emergencies in your bag?"

"Yeah. This thing has saved my life more than once. Well, maybe not my life, but my dignity. Once before I had to give a big presentation in college I went to the bathroom and my fly got stuck in the, ya know, *down* position, but it was all right because I just sewed it up real quick and no one was the wiser."

"Wow."

"And once it got me a date."

"Ooh, do tell."

"I was on an escalator behind a woman and one of the metal panels on the side was warped, so a corner of it stuck out just a little bit far and the edge of her blouse caught it and ripped. When we got to the top I offered to sew it up for her, just so it wouldn't be gaping open while she got to wherever she was going."

"Wow. That is a very boss move."

"Boss? No, not really. I couldn't stop blushing the entire time."

"Well, it worked, didn't it? If it got you the date?"

"Yeah. By the time I'd fixed her up so she could walk around without flashing anybody, she asked me if I had time to get a beer so she could thank me. We actually dated for a couple of weeks."

"That's more than a date! That's a relationship!"

"A mini one, yes."

"So, what happened?"

"Well, she was only in New York for a couple of weeks on business and she ended up going back to Tacoma at the end of the summer and we broke up. I still see her every once in a while when she visits. Just as friends. She's a great person. There. I think that'll do it. I tried to make the stitches really small. It's not professional, but at least there's not a hole there anymore."

"Holy smokes, it's perfect! Thank you! Hey, can you do any sort of fancy sewing?"

"What do you mean?"

"I mean you have a lot of colors of thread there but you made the repair invisible so I'll never remember that it was even there. Add a little design or something."

"Oh. Um. Okay, sure."

"So . . . wait a second. Let me get this straight."

"Hm?"

"Back to the escalator date thing. This random woman you met and felt attracted to, you ended up on a date with, and that date went well enough that you were together for a couple weeks? And it even ended amicably enough that you're still friends?"

"All correct so far."

"Has this happened to you before?"

"What do you mean?"

"I mean have you dated other people to such success?"

"Oh, yeah. I had a girlfriend in college. Also a really great person. She just had her second kid. I sent a bunch of onesies and burp cloths and stuff. We don't hang out really but we're friendly. And there were a couple others here and there. No sweeping love stories though."

"No, no, I'm not looking for sweeping love stories here, I'm just looking for evidence to support my theory."

"What theory?"

"Well, the whole Katie McConnick unrequited-love debacle, and then you were on about how you're such a bad date. All of that made me think you hadn't had, like, *any* romantic successes. So, the whole 'he's a bad date' thing was making sense to me. But, Sam, based on this new evidence, I don't think you're a bad date. I think you're *allergic* to the women your mother picks out for you."

"Um . . ."

"Think about it. Your worst dates have all been with them, right?"

"Well, yes."

"And you already said that they were generally nice people, right? It's not that your mother is somehow only picking out the worst of the bunch, right?"

"Right."

"Well, then based on my incredible skills of deduction and logic and detectivery, I think you get frozen up on these dates *because* your mother set them up."

"I mean . . . maybe?"

"Think about it. You have perfectly fine chemistry with women your mother has nothing to do with, right?"

"Sometimes. Yes . . ."

"Then maybe it's because you chafe against the idea of arranged marriage, which is pretty much what these dates are setting you up for. Or maybe . . . maybe this is some sort of defense mechanism you've set up to keep your mother out of every aspect of your life?"

"Um . . ."

"Oh, boy. That was way too far, wasn't it? I'm sorry. I got carried away. Just . . . blame it on the panic, yeah?"

"No . . . I mean . . . you're probably right. But, whenever someone tells you exactly what your problem is . . . even if they're right . . . you kind of want to disagree, you know?"

"Yes. Of course. Disagree away! Tell me exactly how ridiculous my ridiculous hypothesis is."

". . ."

"Sam?"

"I'm trying to think of counter arguments but I can't. Probably because you're totally right."

"Sorry. That must be very annoying."

"No, no. Don't apologize for your brilliance. Allergic to my mother's interference, huh? Damn. That's . . . so passive of me."

"Well, I've seen you try to be direct with her. It doesn't seem to take very well."

"She's . . . very good at getting her way."

"And you're not?"

"Well, 'my' way is generally very flexible. That way I can sort of always feel like I'm getting my way no matter what happens."

"So, basically, Sam comes last? But he tells himself he's first?"

"Jeez!"

"Sorry, too presumptuous again? My bad."

"If you're not careful I'm going to embroider a thumbs down on your camera case."

"Yes, but from my perspective it would be a thumbs *up*."

"How about a frown, then?"

"Wouldn't the same rule apply? From a different perspective it would be a smile?"

"No way, have you ever seen an upside down frown? It is not a smile. In fact, it's freakily creepy. Here, look, tilt your head that way, I'll tilt my head this way and look at my frown upside down."

"Ah!"

"See? Totally creepy."

"Killer-clown creepy."

"Exactly. That's what I think about whenever I hear the whole turn-your-frown-upside-down thing."

"You think of killer clowns?"

"I try very hard not to spend a lot of time thinking of killer clowns. I live alone, remember? My brain is a clown-free zone for my own mental health. Here. I'm done with the embroidery now. Do you like it?"

"Oh, I love it! What's the meaning behind a green star?"

"The meaning is that I tried to do a shamrock, for good luck, but got confused on where all the leaves should go, so I turned it into a star. If you don't like it I can always tear it out."

"No! No. This is a piece of original art from someone who wished me non-traditional good luck. I'll never tear it out. I'll treasure it. Thank you, Sam. I love it. I'll think of you whenever I see it from now on."

"Oh. Ah. You don't—I mean . . . You're welcome. I—"

"So what are we gonna do about your date allergy?"

"Huh?"

"We've established that you have an allergy to dates your mother sets up. But you've got the biggest date of your life tonight!"

"The biggest date of my life, oh, my God. This is so . . . not that."

"What do you mean? It's a date with your high-school crush. Redemption. Full circle. All that. So, we need to figure out a way for you to crush it tonight. Best date ever."

"And how could we possibly do that? I'm gonna be all busrumpled. Plus first dates are just . . . And she's someone that I've, historically, always been tongue-tied around anyhow. Yeah, the odds are not in my favor."

"Let's practice, then."

"Practice? Practice what?"

"Your date. I'll be Katie."

"Gwen . . ."

"Can't suspend your disbelief that far? Okay, then just pretend I'm a random woman your mother set you up with. We'll start there."

"And for some reason you've agreed to a bus date? You must have very low expectations."

"No, no. We're obviously not on a bus. We're . . . in a tapas restaurant. A really cute one. With candles on each table and colorful tablecloths. There's a singer crooning softly in the corner. We're drinking delicious wine."

". . ."

"Are you *blushing* right now?"

"You described a very romantic setting out of nowhere! You caught me off guard."

"Okay, that's very cute. So, you tell me, what happens next?"

"In the tapas restaurant?"

"Yes. On your blind date in the tapas restaurant."

"Well, if this were real, and you really were someone my mother had just set me up with, I would probably be sweating and trying desperately to think of something to say. Hey, traffic's moving again!"

"I know! Don't jinx it! Well, why don't you ask about the usual things? Job, hobbies, summer plans—that kind of thing."

"And it's just totally fine to ask about all that kinda boring stuff? I mean . . . I'm not supposed to be trying to be . . . sparky?"

"Sparky? No, you can't fake that. No one can force themselves to have a spark. It either happens or it doesn't."

"See? That's my problem. It never *just happens* for me."

"Are you kidding? You're plenty sparky. You've been sparking all over the place. You even embroidered a star on my camera case. What's more sparky than that? I think with these women you shouldn't think of it as sparky, but maybe more . . . flirty? If you're wanting to show interest, that is. If you're not wanting to show interest at all, then just forget it and try to keep the conversation as polite and neutral as possible."

"Oh. Great. A simple directive. Be flirty. There's no way I'll botch that."

"That's why we're practicing! Okay. So. Go!"

"Go?"

"Talk flirty to me."

"Talk . . . you've got to be kidding me. Is there a person on earth who can flirt on command?"

"There are little things you can do to ramp yourself up. Here! I'll show you. Give lots of eye contact while you're talking. Like this. And maybe I might just sort of absently smooth out this wrinkle on your sleeve. Like that. And maybe I'll start to lean in. And see! You automatically leaned in too."

"Oh! Sorry! It was a reflex!"

"That was what I was going for! There are all these little things that you can do to make things flirtier and more fun. And the truth is, when you're on a non-Mom date, you probably do them organically. You just need to practice them a little bit for tonight so you don't get too in your own head."

"I just . . . I'm not sure it works that way."

"What way?"

"I mean, when *you* do those things it creates this . . . atmosphere, right? You made this cozy little world, just the two of us. But . . . if I were to do that . . . Look. I just try hard not to one: stare at women; two: touch them or their clothes without asking; three: crowd them. And that's kind of all the moves you just showed me? I just don't think it has the same flirty effect when a man does it. The last thing I want to be is menacing, you know?"

"Okay . . . I see your point."

“Then why are you laughing?”

“I . . . was trying to picture you as menacing, and . . . you’re just very not that. But, yes, I agree that these moves don’t work in every scenario.”

“Oh, I think your phone is dinging.”

“Hm? Oh . . . UGH!”

“What?”

“It’s freaking Niles Shaw. Look! Read this!”

“*Free for dinner after my interview tonight?* What an asshole! Not only is he claiming he’s gonna get the interview, he’s asking you out at the same time? What a total and complete—”

“I know. He’s the absolute worst. He’s done it like a million times. Look at all the other texts he’s sent me. He’s always asking me out as a way of showing me he’s in the same place as I am, and thus, going to upload a bunch of photos and interviews from that same city to jock my style. A lot of his followers even think we’re dating because we show up in the same locations so much. I think he revels in it.”

“This is . . . this is more than a rival. This is just *weird*.”

“He thinks we have a will they/won’t they thing going.”

“Meaning he thinks it’s, what, *cute* to have stolen your intellectual property?”

“Easy come, easy go. For him. He’s attractive and very rich and I honestly think he kind of fell into these followers. So, he doesn’t really see the big deal in copying me. He thinks that if I hate it so much, I should just change my angle and do something different. Like a business decision.”

“Right. He doesn’t see what he’s doing as creative fulfillment, so he doesn’t see why you would care so much about your project.”

“And he’s just a competitive prick, so no matter what, he wants to do what I do, but better. With more followers and more advertiser engagement.”

"What an absolute turd. Does he have any other enemies?"

"Why?"

"Because you should collaborate with them."

"Ooh! How diabolical."

"But no, I take it back. I think your strategy is better. Just keep ignoring him."

"And, of course, get there first, get this interview and then shove it down his throat."

"Yes. Exactly. Good thing the traffic is moving again."

"Yeah. Things are looking up!"

"Can I ask an . . . extremely ignorant question?"

"Sure."

"Say that Niles Shaw hadn't copied your entire life's work and passed it off as his own."

"Okay . . ."

"He'd kind of be the perfect guy for you, wouldn't he?"

". . ."

"I take it, from the look on your face, that you can't play the what if? game with Niles Shaw. So . . . forget we're talking about Niles Shaw."

"What are we talking about, then?"

"We're talking about a guy who travels the world for his job and does photography and writes and meets people. Isn't that . . . perfect for you?"

"Oh. I see what you're saying. You're asking if I'd want to date someone with the same job as me? Someone who could travel everywhere with me?"

"Yeah."

"Um . . . I don't know. That's never really been an option before. So, I have no idea if I'd like that. I've always just dated people in different cities and seen them when I could see them and then broken up when things got hard."

"And . . . that's the way you like it?"

"That's the way it's been."

"Do you want to get married? Or have kids?"

"You know how you may or may not be allergic to your mom setting you up?"

"Mmhmm?"

"Well, I may or may not be allergic to that question."

"Ah. I see. Sorry. I shouldn't have—"

"*Oh, my God!*"

"*Look out!*"

"*Ahhh!*"

"Gwen? Are you all right? Gwen?"

"I'm . . . I'm okay. Are you okay? What the hell just happened?"

"I think we might have blown out a tire or something."

"The bus just . . . I . . . I've never . . ."

"Me either. I hope everyone is all right. At least we were able to get to the side of the road."

"Sam?"

"Yeah?"

"Thank you for shielding me like that, but . . . I think you can let go of me now."

"Oh. Sorry! Reflex, I think."

"I'm glad you did because I think I would have smacked the hell out my forehead if you hadn't. Thank you."

"All passengers please disembark and wait in the grass at least fifty feet from the bus. Please make sure you take all your belongings with you."

"Wait, Sam. They want us to get off the bus?"

"Apparently."

"And wait on the side of the road."

"I guess so."

"For what?"

"Another bus? Sometimes they have to route another bus from elsewhere to finish the trip."

"This has happened to you before?"

"Never *this* exactly. But once the engine blew and we had to wait for another bus to come."

"How long did it take?"

". . ."

"Sam. How long did it take?"

"It might be different this time."

"Sam."

". . . We waited for about three and a half hours before the bus got there."

"Oh, my God. Sam, I'm so screwed. *I'm so screwed.*"

"No, no. Don't panic. One step at a time. Let's just get off the bus. We'll figure something out, I swear."

Chapter Six

Gwen

Sam doesn't let me carry my bags. He carries everything for me. I mean, I only have the one backpack, but still. He carries everything for Shirley too. All of her knitting bags, her rolly suitcase, and a tie-dye knapsack. There's a back entrance to the bus, one they only open for emergencies, but, yeah, I guess almost spinning off the road in a passenger bus constitutes an emergency because the driver has opened it and Sam hops off the back. I watch through the window as he jogs through pools of spring sunshine to drop off all of our bags in a patch of shade far back from the highway. His hair is a shocking, quenching blue in the sunshine. I'm parched.

Then he's jogging back. There's no staircase, just a three-foot drop to the ground and he's reaching up two hands to Shirley. She goes to him with complete trust and as he lifts her gently down I get a very funny feeling in my chest. It's like the parched feeling is getting . . . more parched.

Picture the cracked red dirt of a desert, nothing but the toasted scent of bone-dry ground for miles. Now full throttle a hairdryer on that same dirt. That's the kind of parched we're talking right now.

I'm next, apparently. He's reaching his hands up to me and for some silly reason, instead of putting my hands in his, I put them on his shoulders. Which means that instead of putting his hands in mine, he puts them on my waist. He lifts me down, my feet touch earth, the cars speed past in a blur, and Sam and I are winter-formal-slow-dance close. We're first-kiss close. We're is-that-your-heartbeat-or-mine? close.

And then, I see them, really look, for the first time. His eyes. Which are dark green and clashing terribly with the indigo hair. It's a handsome kind of clashing, but still, indigo is definitely not his color and something about that is just so endearing that it makes a quick laugh burst from nowhere.

Sam blinks, drops his hands, and steps back. I clear my throat and head in the direction of Shirley, who is already pulling a picnic blanket out of thin air next to our luggage. She and I sit side by side and share a plastic baggie of green grapes (provided by her, of course).

We sit in silence and watch the show. The driver flits frantically from passenger to passenger, alternately confirming that everyone is all right and barking into a cell phone with the bus company. There's a mother with a baby strapped to her chest bouncing in the shade, trying to trigger an impromptu nap. Four or five kids are playing some sort of rubber band skin-snapping game that's making them all laugh hysterically and I wonder if they knew one another before this bus ride. A lovey-dovey couple naps in the sun. A prickly couple stands three feet apart in the shade, looking at their phones.

And through it all, there's Sam. I've officially lost count of how many times he's been off and on the bus. He's hauling luggage, helping people jump down, holding the leash of a dog so tiny in comparison to him it could easily fit inside his shoe. He talks to the driver and figures out how to open the hatches for the under-the-bus storage and then he's literally climbing into the belly of the beast to hoist out trunks and taped-up garbage bags filled with clothes.

"Your man is a *man*."

I turn to see a teenage boy with a silver piercing through the center of his nose standing in the shade behind Shirley and me. He's watching Sam with an appreciative twinkle in his eye.

There's a layer of gleaming sweat on Sam's brow and his T-shirt is starting to stick to him in places. Even from here I can see that his jeans have seen better days but that only makes them love him more. I'm a little befuddled by the view, which might be the reason I thoughtlessly answer with:

"He sure is."

I feel Shirley's eyes on the side of my face and I quickly make an amendment.

"I mean, he's not *my* man. But yeah. He definitely knows how to toss a suitcase around, doesn't he?"

"Oh, you're not together?" the kid asks, pulling out a cigarette and putting it between his lips.

All it takes is a single look from Shirley and he's sheepishly filing the cigarette back in its pack. Oh, to have that kind of firepower.

"I saw that little moment at the back of the bus," he says, "and could have sworn you two were together."

I twist to face him. "You saw that? It was a moment, right? It was totally a moment."

"Definitely."

Sam . . . makes me thirsty. And who could blame me? Not that he and I could ever be a thing. I mean, wasn't he just hitting the nail on the head that my perfect man is basically Niles Shaw minus Niles Shaw? I can't think of someone more different from Niles Shaw than Sam. Homebody 9-to-5er family man. Yeah . . . that would have an ice cube's chance in Mississippi sunshine of working out. I can see it now. I'd spend roughly three months disappointing the hell out of him every time I announced a new trip, and then we'd break up. He didn't even want to make it work long distance with a woman in Tacoma. And that's very different than making it work long distance with a woman who works, well, everywhere. Yeah . . .

One blown tire and now I'm sitting on the side of the road losing time before my big interview, imagining Niles racing a blue streak across the sky, and I'm filing away a new crush under the don't-even-waste-your-time category. What a total sinkhole of a day.

I'm still studying the kid. Besides the nose-piercing, I can see a tattoo peeking up from the collar of his shirt and that *might* be a tongue piercing as well. He's got a sly, interesting face with light brown skin, dark freckles, and coppery hair. And in this sunlight . . .? I would die to photograph him.

I may have just flushed the single biggest opportunity of my career down the drain by choosing the bus today, but that doesn't mean I shouldn't work at *all*. "Hey, I know this is random, but . . . would you have any interest in being featured on my blog?"

I pull it up on my phone and hand it over to him.

"I photograph people and their adornments, like your nose-piercing, and I interview them about when and why and how they chose it. If you have any—"

"This is *your* blog?" he asks, his eyes going perfectly round. "Are you kidding me? I've been following you for years. I'm Castor, by the way."

"Oh. Great! Castor, are you intere—"

"YES. Right now? You want to do it right now?"

"Sure. Let me just get my camera out."

Chapter Seven

Sam

I'm hauling a suitcase containing approximately seventy-five pounds of rocks out of the bus and onto the grass when I see it. Gwen working. She's positioning a kid in the sunshine and smiling, coaching him on how to tip his face. Something glitters in the middle of his nose. She's on a slight hill so she crouches down as she backs up, one of her legs stretched out below her and the other bent up underneath her. She's fluid and flexible, the camera moving naturally as she snaps a few shots. She says something, the kid cracks up and she takes a few more photos.

I feel dizzy when I crawl back into the belly of the hot bus to get, thank God, the last remaining suitcase. This was technically the bus driver's, Jerry's, job. But I've known him peripherally for years from these bus rides and he's got to be at least sixty. So, whatever, I can kick my own ass for a day and help make this process a little easier for him.

As soon as I've hoisted the suitcase out, I lean back against the bus and consider my options. Because now that I'm the bus driver's favorite person on earth, I've just been treated to some insider info.

The earliest the relief bus could possibly arrive will be two hours. Which would make Gwen an hour late for her interview. And certainly at least an hour behind Shaw.

And there she is over there. Dancing around with a camera, positively glowing, and I just want to make everything work for her.

It might be a little bit of a thing.

Gwen gives off a very "I've got this handled on my own" vibe, which I like. A lot. But . . . for some reason I feel vaguely responsible for her sitting on the side of the road while this incredible opportunity slips through her fingers.

I know that's ridiculous. I'm just a passenger on this bus. I'm not a mechanic or even the driver. But I'm so familiar with this route, have taken this exact bus so many times (I can tell because the carpet is mismatched in the aisle, so I always know when it's this particular bus) that it feels almost like I've personally failed Gwen. Imagine if you had a faulty bathroom lock in your home and Gwen got locked in and it caused her to miss a professional opportunity that had the potential to change the course of her life. You'd feel responsible, right? Well, the feeling I'm having right now is some cousin to that feeling.

I'm *compelled* to help.

I wrack my brain.

As I lean against the bus, trying to get my sweat glands to stop basking in their five minutes of fame, I pull out my phone. First things first, I check a few taxi and ride-share apps. The taxi options are twice as expensive as a plane ticket would have been and I quickly file those away as a last resort. The ride-share options are much more reasonable in price but none of them are immediate pick-you-up-on-the-side-of-the-highway sort of situations. Which leaves . . . hitch-hiking? We'd be less likely to get picked up as a pair but no way would I want her to hitch-hike by herself. If the two of us are together, she'll be way safer.

I crane my head to try to see which exit we're closest to. If we can walk to a gas station, we could try to talk someone into giving us a ride.

The green and white exit sign is a beacon in the sun about two hundred yards down and I think I might be misreading it. There's no way we're at that exit. That would be way too serendipitous.

"Hey, Jerry?" I quickly check with him to make sure we're near the town I think we are and he confirms it.

Before I do anything else, I need to confirm this idea is good with Gwen. Because the last thing I want to do is pressure or intimidate her. I'm trying to make things better here, not worse.

But the bottom line is this:

She's really gonna have to trust me.

Chapter Eight

"Hey there, macho man."

"Me?"

"Yeah, you. Who else has been slinging luggage and sweating in the sunshine for the last twenty minutes."

"I . . . don't think I've ever been called a macho man before."

"How does it feel?"

"Um. Surreal. Where's Shirley?"

"She went to flirt her way into some grape soda from that old guy over there. I think it's really working for her."

"Hey, you seem awfully relaxed for someone who's stranded on the side of the road."

"I've accepted my situation. This just wasn't the right opportunity for me. It wasn't in the cards. Fate had its way. Well, I should say I've *almost* accepted the situation. I haven't called to cancel the appointment yet, but I guess I should do that now. I don't want to be rude."

"Wait! I . . . have an idea."

"Okay . . ."

"It's just an idea, so if you say no, for any reason, that's totally fine."

"Lay it on me."

"Well, you know, fate might not be as cruel as you think it is, because our bus broke down right outside the exit for

Sturbridge. And I happen to have a friend who lives there. And he happens to have a car."

". . . Are you saying that your friend might just give up his Sunday afternoon at the drop of a hat and give us a ride all the way down to New York City? I dunno, seems like a long shot to me."

"Long shot or not, if I can get him to do it, would you accept the ride?"

"Are you kidding me? I'll *pay him* for the ride. I'll sing Billy Joel songs the whole way there if he wants me to. I'll ride in the trunk if I have to. Sam, if you could seriously get me to New York in time for this interview there's nothing—I'll be forever—I can't even—Okay, so maybe I have not, *in any way*, accepted this situation. Apparently. Wow."

"Okay, *great*, that's exactly the answer I was hoping for. Let me call him real quick, all right?"

"Yes, please."

"Hey, Danny, it's Sam . . . Yeah . . . Yeah. How are you? . . . Oh, yeah? That's great . . . She's good, man . . . Yeah. She's making it, still pretty torn up after the break-up. And this weekend was obviously really hard for her, but she'll be all right. Listen. My bus broke down right outside of exit 62 on CT-15. And a friend and I really need to get to Manhattan as soon as possible. Do you still have your car? . . . Well, the day has finally come, man. I'm officially calling in *the* favor . . . Yup. Is it possible? Can you do it? . . . Excellent. I don't think it would be safe for you to get us off the side of the highway, so if we walk to the nearest gas station, could you meet us? . . . Perfect. We'll be there in ten minutes."

"Sam! What the hell was that?!"

"It worked."

"It just *worked*?! I don't—I can't—we officially have a ride to New York City right now?"

"What's going on, kiddos?"

"Shirley, Sam just got us a ride to the city! In a car."

"Yeah. Only there's a problem."

"What's that?"

"Apparently he's storing a bunch of crap in his car and there are only two seats available."

"Oh."

"Yeah. Look, Danny's a really good guy. I can vouch for him. You two will be perfectly safe with him, I swear."

"Sam. Dear."

"Yes?"

"I'm not going. You're going."

"But—"

"Yes, yes, you're a gentleman and we all love you for it, but I'm not driving in some strange car with a bunch of kids. I'm going to wait here for the replacement bus like a good old lady, all right? I'm comfortable in the shade and I just made a man friend. So, go on without me, kids. You and Gwen have a good time on your adventure, all right?"

"Shirley, you saved my number, right? It's Gwen, last name C-E-L-L-A-R, like a basement. You got it, right? And you won't forget to text me?"

"I won't. We'll have tea next week. I'll curl my hair and wear my best skirt. You won't even recognize me. Now go on and catch your ride!"

"Bye, Shirley!"

"Goodbye, Shirley. Next time we're on the same bus let's sit together, all right?"

"You got it, son. You can flush my homemade peanut brittle down the toilet again."

"I—"

"Sam, we've really gotta go. Bye, Shirley!"

"Bye, Gwen!"

"Bye, Shirley! See you in the city! Oh! And bye, Castor. Talk to you soon!"

"Later, Gwen!"

"You made a friend."

"I think I made a lot of friends, actually."

"I think he likes you. He's still looking this way."

"Actually, I think he likes *you*."

"Oh. Ah . . . really?"

"Yeah, he said you were a *man*, and I'm pretty sure he was using all caps in his brain."

"Gosh, is there something in the water today? Why is everyone talking about my manhood?"

"Sam, you've saved like a hundred lives today, and flexed your muscles a ton. On a bus. Oh, shit! You're basically Keanu!"

"Oh, my God. That's . . . I don't even . . ."

"Come on, admit you're Keanu so that I can be Sandra. I've always wanted to be Sandra Bullock."

"Here, walk on this side of me. Away from the speeding cars."

"Why? Because *you're* somehow able to survive getting hit by a car? Using nothing but your pulsing manhood?"

"Oh, now my manhood is pulsing? Can't I just be an ordinary citizen like everyone else?"

"Some of us were born to be heroes, Sam."

"You can be the hero, all right? I'll just . . . be your cheering section."

"Is that the gas station where we're meeting your friend?"

"Yup. And I'm sorry to say that *that* is the car we'll be riding in."

"Sorry? Why? It's beautiful. The most beautiful car I've ever seen. Don't insult the car that is saving my life."

"I guess we'll just agree on the fact that it has a lot of character."

"So, what's this big favor you called in? It sounded like a big deal between you."

"Oh. Ah. Nothing. It's nothing really. Just an old thing from childhood."

"You're really not going to tell me?"

"Like I said, it's nothing. Not even an interesting story . . . *Hey, man!*"

"Sam! My dude! Bring it in, bring it in. Let's bro-hug it out. And who is this?"

"Hi, I'm Gwen."

"Hey, Gwen, I'm Danny. Nice to meet you. So . . . you must be pretty important to my dude here if he's finally calling in this favor after twenty years."

"Funny you should mention that because your *dude* won't explain a single thing to me about this so-called favor."

"We really don't have to get into specifics . . ."

"You didn't tell her the story, Sam? Come on, man, you have to tell her the story."

"Gwen, it's really not—"

"You could tell me all about it on the ride, Danny. I can't wait to hear every sordid detail."

"Oh. Uh . . . I'm not going with you."

"Huh?"

"I told you, man. There are only two seats."

"Oh, I thought you meant there was only room for two *passengers*."

"No, two people total. The driver and one passenger. The entire back seat is full. See? That's pretty much my entire kitchen in there."

"Hold on, are you *moving* today?"

"Yeah."

"And you're still willingly just giving us your car today?"

"Hey, I finally got the chance to be out of debt to this favor. I'm not missing this opportunity. Just don't get any parking tickets in the city, yeah? I, um, might have a few outstanding already. And btw I didn't have time to fill her up. Lemme just grab my bike off the bike rack and . . . yeah, that'll do it. You kids have fun."

"I'll drive it back up after work tomorrow, yeah?"

"Nah, don't worry about it. I'm taking a train into the city to see a concert on Wednesday so just keep it and I'll drive it home then."

"But you said your entire kitchen is in the back seat!"

"I'll eat takeout. No worries! Keys are in the ignish. Later!"

"Thank you, Danny! I know we just met, but I love you! You have no idea what this means to me! . . . And just like that, he's gone."

"He's a bit of an odd duck, but he's really good people."

"Ya think? This is, like, the most needlessly generous thing anyone has ever done for me. Well, I mean, I guess he did it for *you*, but still, this is off the charts."

"I'll fill up the tank."

"Okay, I'll grab snacks. Are you hungry? What're you hungry for?"

"Anything I can safely eat while driving."

"Done."

Chapter Nine

"Are you taking pictures of the bus?"

"Yeah. It's times like these I'm glad I'm a professional photographer. I just wanted a couple shots of her through the back window. There she goes. Our not-so-faithful steed."

"She did her best."

"I love your loyalty to Megabus. It's very endearing."

"Doesn't make sense to talk shit about something I heavily rely on twelve times a year. What're you taking pictures of now?"

"Danny's kitchen in our back seat. It's not every day you make a drive with a box full of chef's knives balancing behind your head. Don't crash, okay?"

"Yeah, I'll do my best. Any chance you could shift those boxes around so the knives *aren't* near our heads?"

"Good idea . . . *Dang, that's heavy.* Okay. Done. Now it's a box of oven mitts and dishtowels by our heads."

"Much better."

"So, you're really not going to elaborate on this mysterious favor?"

"Next topic."

"Okay . . . since you're withholding tantalizing information . . . instead, can I take your picture?"

"You want a picture of me?"

"Sure."

"Doing what?"

"Driving. Just whatever you're naturally doing. You don't have to pose or anything."

"And if I let you take a picture of me, you'll stop asking about the favor?"

"For now."

"Um. Okay. Go ahead."

"Sam?"

"Yeah?"

"I said you *don't* have to pose. You can go ahead and drop the peace sign."

"Right. Sorry."

"Just drive. Forget I'm here."

"You're the only other person in the car. How am I supposed to forget you're—Oh, don't take pictures while I'm *talking.* Those are sure to be attractive."

"It's not about taking attractive pictures. It's about taking natural pictures. Catching you in your relaxed, usual movements. That's when the photos get good."

"Will you—are you going to use any of these for your blog?"

"Oh. No. I don't think so. The blog is about strangers."

"And we aren't strangers?"

"I'm pretty sure we're friends."

"Ah. Okay. Friends. Cool."

"But, if I *were* to do a blog post about you, I definitely know what question I'd ask you."

"What's that?"

"So, what's the deal with the hair?"

"Huh?"

"I mean, you've never dyed it before, right?"

". . . right . . ."

"So, a thirty-ish-year-old man who has never dyed his hair

before, suddenly, out of nowhere, dyes his hair a vibrant and unusual color, that he might have to dye back for work, like, three days later . . . there's gotta be some kind of story there, right?"

"Well . . . yeah. I guess there is."

"It wasn't just a style choice?"

"Definitely not."

"So, what's the story?"

"Well . . . how to explain this . . .? Let's just say that my mother . . . thrives . . . when she has something related to me to focus her energy on. And I thought a tattoo might push her over the edge. So, dyed hair it is."

"Let me get this straight. You *purposefully* provided your mother with something to nag you about?"

"Nutshell. Yeah."

". . . I heard you mention to Danny that this was a really tough weekend for her?"

"Yeah. She's been going through this really messy break-up."

"Oh, no."

"It's been her only relationship since my dad. And they were together for a long time. Six or seven years. She even found this ring that he was going to propose to her with, so she was waiting, all excited over that, and then out of the blue he dumped her. It's been really terrible. She's been a little . . . unpredictable since then. I've just been trying to be an even keel for her."

"Except for the blue hair."

"Well, like I said, she does better when she's not bored. And blue hair was . . . not boring for her. I haven't seen her that lively in a while. She was researching cults and quizzing me on whether or not I've been sucked into one. It was nice."

"That *does* sound really nice."

"Ha ha. I know we're weird."

"No, I'm serious. It sounds like the two of you really care

about one another. Everyone's relationships are weird if you look closely enough at them. I have a theory that if your relationship with someone isn't weird, you don't know them well enough yet."

"Oh. Interesting. Actually that rings true to me. I think all of my closest relationships have a bit of an oddity to them."

"So, this guy she was with. Did you like him?"

". . . Um?"

"I'm gonna take that as a no."

"He's fine, I guess. And I tried my hardest not to do the whole 'you'll never be my father' thing. I was in my early twenties when they got together after all. And I wanted—want—my mom to have companionship. She's happier with companionship."

"Who isn't?"

"Right? But . . . he's just sort of flat. I always wondered where the romance was. Not everybody needs or wants romance, and that's cool. Some people just want a buddy. But I know for a fact that my mom wants a real romance. Our house is stuffed full of romance novels and romcom DVDs. And you know how she is with setting me up on blind dates. She's obsessed with romantic stories. But the two of them never went on dates. Or even celebrated anniversaries or anything like that. For Christmas or her birthday he'd always get her something practical that she already needed. Like a new filter for her window air-conditioning unit."

"That's an actual example?"

"Yeah."

"Oh, boy."

"And I just . . . want something more for her. I want her to be . . . fulfilled. And you never really know what goes on in the interior of someone else's relationship, but it never seemed to me that he was able to do that for her."

"Oh, Sam."

"Hm?"

"You're *so* adorable."

"Oh, *God*. That's . . . not what I generally go for. I think I prefer the pulsing manhood angle. Adorable? Yikes."

"No! No, listen. I mean that in the literal sense. Not the way people say it to puppies and babies and stuff. I mean that you are worthy of *adoration*. I don't know if I've ever met somebody more adoration-able. It's absurd to me that you've been dating around for so long and aren't in a relationship. What's wrong with these women? Katie McConnick is in for the thrill of a lifetime at the bus station this evening. Oh! Wait! Oh no!"

"What?"

"You're not going to *be* at the bus station this evening!"

"Huh?"

"You're gonna be dropping me off on the Upper East Side instead. You're going to miss your big date!"

"Oh. Right. My big date."

"What're we gonna do? This is terrible!"

"You're really torn up about this?"

"We're talking emotional resolution after more than a decade. This is a big deal."

"You really want me to go on this date?"

"Sam, it's Katie McConnick."

"You don't even know her!"

"She's legendary."

"If you say so."

"Can you text Katie and explain?"

"My mom won't give up her contact info because she still suspects that I'll cancel the date."

"Gimme your phone. I'll text your mom as you and explain the bus situation. She's bound to change the terms of the date with such a good excuse, right?"

"Oh. Maybe. You can give it a shot. You might be in for a

surprise. She's pretty much the most stubborn person I've ever met. Here."

"Your mom is in your phone as 'Ma'?"

"Yeah. Is that weird?"

"No, probably not."

"What are your parents in your phone as?"

"Their first and last names. I'm probably the weird one now that I think about it. 'Ma'. This is so cute. Okay . . . here's the text strand and—"

"Gwen? You all right?"

"You . . . texted your mom about me?"

"I—oh, shit, wait! Don't read that. Give it back."

"Wait, let me see! What did you say about me?"

"Gwen, I'm driving! Stop stiff-arming my face!"

"Then let the phone go!"

"No way. I—there."

"Hey, you locked it."

"Yes."

"Unlock it!"

"Literally never."

"Ugh! What the heck! What happened to the accommodating man I've come to know and love? Accommodate me! I demand you accommodate me!"

"I'm pulling a very rare move and putting my foot down. You will not be accommodated."

". . ."

"Are you mad that I'm not accommodating you?"

". . ."

"Did you just stick your tongue out at me?"

"Perhaps."

"Okay, fine. How much did you see?"

"I saw my name, that's it."

"Okay. My mother wanted to know your name. So I told her."

"And how did your mother know I even existed enough to *have* a name in the first place?"

". . ."

". . ."

". . ."

"Hey, Sam, are you hungry?"

"Oh. Um. Yeah, actually I am. What did you get for us?"

"The snacks were surprisingly thin on the ground, but there was this little tiny taco truck parked out back so I got us some food from there."

"Oh. Wow!"

"Yeah. But they were out of wraps of all kinds so I had to get us taco salads."

"Oh."

"Is that bad?"

"No, I mean, it sounds delicious. But it also sounds like maybe the hardest possible thing to eat while driving?"

"Uh huh. I'll feed it to you."

"Oh. Ah. Okay."

"Here . . . let me just . . . there, all right. Smells good, doesn't it?"

"Yes."

"And here's your bite . . . psych!"

"Did you just fake me out?!"

"Yes. You can get this bite of delicious taco salad when you explain what you were texting your mother about."

". . . You're cruel."

"Yes."

"And scary."

"Sure."

"This is pure manipulation."

"It's for a good cause."

"That cause being?"

"My insatiable curiosity."

". . ."

"Come on, Sam. If you saw that I was texting someone about you, wouldn't you want to know what I'd said?"

"Oh, fine. You win. I texted my mom and told her that I wouldn't be answering any more phone calls while I was on the bus. And she wanted to know why. I explained that I was sitting next to someone that I wanted to talk to instead of talking on the phone. And she wanted to know about you."

"And? What'd you tell her?"

"I told her you were a photographer and a writer and that you were based in NYC. And I told her your name. But that was about an hour ago, so you can bet that she knows more about you than I do, at this point."

"You think she googled me?"

"Are you kidding me? You were sitting next to her precious son on a bus, you're lucky if she didn't hire a PI to investigate you."

"What's your mom's name?"

"Brenda."

"Damn, Brenda's intense."

"That she is."

"Wait, what's your last name?"

"Oh. It's, ah, Champion."

"Your last name is Champion?"

"Yup."

"You sound embarrassed about that."

"No, it's just that telling people my last name usually ends up being a *thing*. And it's kind of a mind fuck to have the last name Champion when you've never won a single thing in your life."

"Yet."

"Huh?"

"You haven't won anything *yet*."

"What kinds of things do adults win? Aren't all the opportunities to win stuff when you're young?"

"Well, there's the MacArthur Genius Grant."

"Not likely."

"Nobel? Science? Peace? Poetry?"

"Brain not smart."

"Okay, how about the Oscars? Tonies? Grammies? Emmies?"

"Ah, yes. Of course. How could I have ever counted those out."

"I mean, there are always moral victories. You seem like the kind of guy who wins those."

"Thanks? I think that may have been the meanest thing anyone has ever said to me. Have I earned any taco salad yet?"

"Oh! Sorry. Yes. Here."

"Yum."

"Oh, wow. We're actually making good time."

"Well, I think the bus goes pretty far below the speed limit usually. This is more of a reasonable pace."

"Oh, my gosh. I think we're actually gonna get there in time!"

"I think we just might."

"Okay, if there's any world where we have a second to spare, we have to find somewhere to pull over so that I can change my outfit."

"I thought you only had the tux, the tuna pants, and some hubba hubba pjs."

"I have one more outfit but it's the only acceptable thing I have to wear for the interview so I didn't want to change into it and then sit in the tuna seat again."

"Aaaaand, it's a good thing you didn't."

"Why?"

"Taco salad went splat."

"Ahhhhh, damn!"

"Sorry about that."

"No, it's not your fault. I'm the one who bought taco salad for a road trip."

"I'll pay for your dry-cleaning bill . . . What's that look for?"

"Why would you pay for my dry-cleaning bill?"

"Well, it was *my* tuna sandwich."

"That's true, but I will not be dry-cleaning an old pair of jeans. They can get clean for a dollar twenty-five at the laundromat around the corner with all the rest of my clothes."

"Okay, well the tux'll need dry-cleaning then."

"And why would you pay for it?"

"Because the taco salad splatted when you were in the middle of feeding me!"

"Not really the middle, I wouldn't say. More like the tail end. I don't think I've ever seen someone eat faster than that. My arm could barely keep up."

"Well, someone sat on my sandwich earlier so I was pretty hungry."

"You know, it's getting a little *cheeky* over there on the drivers' side of the car."

"Hey, you never answered my question from earlier."

"Which question?"

"Whether or not you've ever been on a blind date. You know pretty much every detail about my dating life at this point and I know nothing about yours. Except that Matt Judd was a dick when he was a teenager."

"Yeah, but he was so hot."

"Noted."

"You actually care about this topic?"

"Didn't we already establish that insatiable curiosity is taken gravely seriously in this car?"

"Well . . . the answer to the blind-date question is no. I

mean . . . I've been on impromptu dates with people I'd just met. But no one has ever set me up on a date before. And *certainly* no family member has ever set me up on a date before."

"You sound . . . bummed about that?"

"Do I?"

"Do you wish your family would set you up?"

". . ."

"Sorry, am I being nosy?"

"No. Well, yes. But you're . . . doing the thing again."

"The Dory thing? Making you tell your secrets because I'm just a rando on a bus? Well, I guess at this point that last thing doesn't apply. I'm not a rando on a bus anymore."

"Yeah . . . and the weird thing is that I think you're getting me to tell my secrets because you're actually a friend in a car. I . . . don't talk about my family. Ever, really."

". . . Why?"

"Well, this isn't quite the fun dating topic that you'd proposed, but . . . I think . . . my family might just be the opposite of your mother."

"How so?"

"Well, Brenda seems to, ah, manage you quite a bit, right?"

"Definitely."

"Well, my family has absolutely no *idea* what to do with me. They've never tried to manage me a second of my life. In fact, they pretty much all stand back about twenty feet with their hands raised."

"They're scared of you?"

"No? I don't think so? They just . . . I'm very different from them. There are my parents, who met at eighteen and got married at twenty-four –the second my dad came home from the army. And then there's my sister, who met her husband at eighteen and married him while he was still on active duty. And now they live, literally, on the same block as my parents and have four kids. They all have dinner together four or five nights a week. My sister and my mom share clothes and scour yard sales together. My dad and my brother-in-law play in a softball league for veterans together. And none of that is a bad thing, obviously. In fact, it gives me a lot of peace of mind knowing that they all mesh together so well and take care of one another. If my sister didn't like yard sales then who would my mom spend her Saturday afternoons with, you know? If my brother-in-law didn't play softball, then who would drive my dad to and from games? I guess it's just kind of like they all speak a language together and I need the subtitles to know what's going on. I'm the odd one out . . . Guess what I do when I'm with them?"

"Hm?"

"I try and fail to think of topics and can only think about how long the passing silence is becoming. Sound familiar? At least your awkwardness only extends to strangers and not your immediate family."

"Oh, Gwen."

"Yeah. They are not curious about my life in the least. Where I've just been, where I'm going next . . . it all just *exhausts* them. I don't think my dad has ever even seen my blog. They think spending money on a New York rent is ridiculous. They think having a roommate at age thirty is ridiculous. They think the fact that I bought a camera instead of a car is ridiculous. They think it's so weird that I'm not married. And they cannot *imagine* what kind of man would ever want to marry me. They worry I won't have kids and that I'll regret it when I'm old. They worry I *will* have kids and then I'll be this unpredictable mother who takes my kids overseas and has them go to school in other countries and never knows when the next paycheck will be coming in."

"I'm so sorry."

"The thing about someone setting you up on a blind date? There's a lot that actually goes into that, even if the date ends up being a bust. They have to know you well enough to think, would this person go with that person? What is this person looking for in a mate? Would they have a nice time together? Are they looking for the same thing in a partner? And then the kicker? The most important part? You actually have to *care* about the future of the person you're setting up on a date. Your mother, micromanager that she is, knows that you ultimately would like to be married with children, right? So she's clumsily doing her part to make that happen. I honestly think it's kind of nice. I mean, I totally understand why you'd want it to stop. But it also shows just how much she cares about you. It shows the pains she'll undergo to ensure your future. And . . . I'm jealous of that. I've never had that."

"I can't imagine someone not being interested in you, Gwen. You lead such an interesting life."

"Interesting, yeah. But exhausting too. I . . . guess I understand why . . . Look, I'm not pretending that I'm, like, a stellar family member either. But I try to keep up on their hobbies and job promotions and whatnot. Whenever we talk it's because I call."

"You were with them last night? At the family reunion shindig?"

"Yeah. It wasn't technically a reunion. But the whole family was there."

"And . . . how'd it go?"

"None of them seemed to care very much that I was there, other than the fact that it was extremely important I was there, you know?"

"Um. No. You lost me."

"My attendance was required. But once I was there, no one cared."

"Ah, I see. They didn't want you to miss it for reasons other than your dazzling company."

"Yup. And I just kind of sat there and then stood there and then sat again and ate food and went home. Then this morning when I got the call from my editor that I needed to come home for the interview, I got a huge guilt trip from my mom and my sister that I was leaving a day early and we hadn't gotten to spend any time together yet. Even though we all shared a table last night. And ugh. Sorry. I've now crossed over into venting territory."

"That's okay. You can vent. Venting is necessary. Good for your blood pressure. Let it out."

"Venting makes me feel like a whiner."

"You know when you turn the shower on but you don't put the pressure up all the way and it makes that high pitch squeal?"

"Sure."

"Well, I think that's kind of what whining is. It's when you have feelings but you don't open the valve all the way, so it all just kind of pitifully squeaks out. I personally think it feels better to just open the gate the whole way and let it all come pouring out. Then, it's over faster and you feel empty and cleaned out afterward. The only downside is that sometimes there's a little wreckage."

"I really can't imagine you letting your feelings out full throttle, come what may. You seem like a very self-contained person."

"Well, I don't have a temper, if that's what you mean. And it only happens once in a blue moon. And I try really hard to vent to someone who has nothing to do with the situation so that they're not caught in the crossfire. I vent about work to my mom. Vent about my mom to my friends. That kind of thing."

"Tell me more about your friends."

"No, no. We were talking about you, remember? You only

answered the blind-date question. Not any of the other dating stuff."

"You actually care about that?"

"Doesn't everyone care about other people's dating lives?"

"All right, well, put on your seat belt."

"Oh, it's that intense of a ride?"

"Boyfriends in every city I travel to. Sugar daddies out the wazoo. I've got an OnlyFans on the side and more regular booty calls than my phone currently has storage for."

". . ."

"Sam."

". . ."

"Sam, I was kidding."

"Oh. Ah. Right. About which part?"

"All of it except for one thing. I'll let you decide which the one thing is."

"Well, if the one thing is an OnlyFans page, I'm sure my mother already knows about it and will be informing me of it via text any moment."

"Brenda's out here keeping her baby on the up and up."

"Wait, are you serious? The one thing was actually an OnlyFans? It's cool if it is, I'll probably just have a lot of follow-up questions because I've never met someone who does the webcam thing before."

"No, the one true thing was the sugar-daddy thing. But it was only one guy. Not guys out the wazoo and it was only for like a *minute*."

". . . More information, please."

"He was this older French gentleman that I met in Belgium and we were sort of together for like a month and a half."

"And he . . . paid for everything?"

"Yup. And bought me a ton of presents and stuff."

"Sounds like a dream come true?"

"For some people, yeah. But for me, well, I was getting antsy, wanting to leave Belgium and keep traveling and it was definitely an in-person sort of relationship. So, we ended things. He was a really good boyfriend, though. If I'd been in a less travel-hungry stage we might have stayed together."

"Do you consider your travel hunger to be a stage? It sounds pretty intrinsic to me."

"I love that we just established that I've had a relationship with a sugar daddy and your follow-up questions are about my inclinations to travel."

"Oh. Well. To be fair I have questions about everything. I want to know it all."

"Okay . . . the wanderlust thing . . . I don't think it's a *stage*, necessarily. Because that kind of diminishes it, you know? Makes it this silly little thing that I wanted in my youth, you know?"

"Your youth? You can't be much over thirty. I think you still have your youth."

"Well, let's just say the youthiest parts of my youth, then."

"Got it."

"I've always wanted to travel, my whole life. And not, like, a vacation here or there."

"The thirty-hour car rides to Albuquerque didn't scratch the itch for you?"

"Actually, I think that might have been what started it? I'm not sure. But as long and miserable as those car rides were, it was so fascinating to me to see the landscape change state by state. To hear accents change and feel the climates change with each rest stop we'd get out at. Albuquerque is *very* different from the Hudson Valley. I think it woke me up to the fact that there's a whole, wide world out there."

"That makes sense to me. It sparked your curiosity."

"Definitely. When I graduated high school, I really hadn't

traveled much at all, besides those family trips, and it was the number one thing I wanted to do. My parents wanted me to go to college and they figured if I still had the travel bug I could do a semester abroad or something. But I really didn't want that. I'd never loved being in an academic setting and school was going to have to be on my dime and the debt just loomed over my head. I thought, if I'm going to spend all that money, why shouldn't it be on something I love?"

"Huh."

"That's funny?"

"No, not in a ha ha sort of way. It's just that I had the exact same thought, because I had to pay for my own school as well. But my brain went the opposite direction. It was *If I'm going to spend all that money, it better be for something that is going to prepare me for the workforce so that I can pay back all that money.*"

"I mean, that's very practical."

"Yeah, I've almost paid back all my loans at this point. But you . . . you never had any loans to start with, huh?"

"Right."

"That's also very practical."

"Literally no one has ever referred to my life choices as practical before."

"Keep going with the story. You were in a stalemate with your parents about school . . ."

"Well, it was more of an active-fire situation than a stalemate. But yeah, I knew that I needed to come up with a solution they could get on board with. So, I joined Habitat for Humanity and built houses for a while."

"Oh, *cool.* I've always thought that was *so cool.*"

"It was a great opportunity. I traveled domestically mostly. To places in the Tornado Alley that would get messed up during the bad-weather seasons. And from there I started working on farms here and there for room and board, using this certain website. And once you have a good standing on the website, other places really want you, so then I was getting offers from international farms. And I was off to the races. I kept a very small room in this big house in Brooklyn with a bunch of my Habitat for Humanity friends, but for the most part I was a few months here and then a few months there, landing back in BK in between."

"Picking up odd jobs to pay the bills."

"Mhmm. And then I fell in love with photography and the odd jobs were able to get fewer and farther between."

"And then you met a sugar daddy."

"Aaaand we're back to the sugar daddy."

"In my mind his name is like, Luc, and he has a great head of snow-white hair with a bottlebrush mustache and he drinks brandy on a balcony overlooking Paris."

"Wrong on every count."

"I see why you wouldn't want to refer to your wanderlust as a phase. It seems like it's been a pretty important part of who you are and how you live."

"It . . . is."

"Is there a 'but' in there?"

"Huh? No. No buts. It is what it is."

"Ugh. It is what it is . . ."

"You don't like that phrase?"

"No, it's not that I don't like it. I just don't get any peace from it. It's definitely one that I use to describe my own life, but it makes me more bummed than anything else, I think."

"Is your life a bummer? It doesn't seem like it from the outside, but please, do tell."

"No, it's not a bummer. It's just very . . . regimented. And predictable. Sometimes I think I could do with a little less direction."

"And a little more wanderlust?"

"Um . . . maybe. I mean, the firm direction of my life has been pretty necessary, at least up until this point. The student loans thing is very real. And my mom is very real. She gets an all right pension in her retirement. And she and my dad were careful. She finished paying off their mortgage about ten years ago. So, that's something. But if there were any sort of emergency, medical or otherwise, it would be me taking care of her. There really isn't anyone else. And she's getting older. So, yeah, that day is going to come due at some point, you know? I have just always wanted to be ready for it. So, every day, I get up and go to work and try not to complain. Because I'm grateful to have a job in the first place. I'm grateful I know where my next paycheck will come from. And soon enough, I won't have these loans to think about anymore. And maybe, maybe I can start to think about . . . getting lost a little bit?"

". . ."

"What are you thinking about? You have the funniest expression on your face right now."

"When you're someone's boyfriend, do you just turn into the biggest baby?"

"I . . . what?"

"Sorry for the left-field question, but I was just thinking . . . you keep everything together in all aspects of your life. So neat and tidy and surefooted. You take care of everyone. Certainly your mother, but also strangers on the bus. You're texting your friend trying to find her a place to live . . ."

"And somehow that means that as a boyfriend I must be a total baby?"

"No! It's just that sometimes in romantic relationships people turn into the one thing they can't be anywhere else in their lives. They try to get their needs met. So, are you into, like, the domineering type who plan out every date and tell you what to order at restaurants? You must like someone who takes care of everything for you. So that you can finally relax."

"By that logic you must be into total homebodies who never ever want to go out or do anything fun and only like to eat Hamburger Helper on the couch while they watch reruns of old TV shows they've already seen."

"That was . . . vivid."

"And false, I presume."

"So, you're saying I was completely wrong about what kind of boyfriend you are?"

"The taking care of people thing . . . It's not a response to the kind of life I live, I don't think. I really think it's who I am. So, no. I don't think that I turn into a big baby when I'm with someone. But . . . I do like to be taken care of a bit in return. I mean, that comes in a lot of different forms. After all, you just fed me taco salad. That was nice."

"You're driving me to NYC out of the goodness of your heart. It was the least I could do."

"If I were a big baby, I'd have made you feed me taco salad while *you* were driving. See? I know how to give and take."

"Well, the joke would have been on you because I don't know how to drive a stick shift. Especially not one manufactured in 1982."

"Yes, this car is requiring a bit of a special touch."

"No kidding. This baby is vintage. It's been forever since I've even seen a tape deck. And he doesn't even have an adapter or anything. Do you think he actually listens to tapes?"

"Look around and see if you can find any. But it wouldn't surprise me if he did. Danny is very old school. He only uses an ancient desktop. He still has dial-up internet."

"You're kidding. That's still an option?"

"Well, apparently he's moving, so I don't know what his set-up will be at his new place. But yeah. If it ain't broke don't fix it is definitely his motto. His parents are very keep-up-with-the-Joneses sort of people and he evolved in a very different direction. He doesn't like to have a lot of material tethers. He likes to have a free mind."

"I'm liking this guy more and more. Oh! Jackpot! Here's a whole box of cassettes."

"Anything good?"

"I can't tell. None of them are labeled. Do you think they're all mixes?"

"No idea. Put one in."

"Okay . . . I choose . . . this one. It has a little blue heart sticker on it."

"Jezebel, I love you, baby. Every song on this
tape made me think of you. For this first song,
remember that time in the Poconos?
When the power went out and we had to
survive on nothing but body heat and our lo—"

"Oh, my God, Sam!"

"Wow."

"So . . . I take it Jezebel is Danny's girlfriend?"

"Former. Like, a million years ago. Fast forward and see if you can't find the music."

"I'll never forget those hot nights, girl."

"Oh no."

"We were burning up the sheets."

"No, no, no."

"I really want to hear the songs, but I'm too scared of your friend's narration in between."

"Same. Let's bail on this tape and choose another."

"Okay . . . how about this one."

"Betty, I love you, baby. Every song on this tape made me think of you. I chose this first song because I'll never forget the way you looked that first night in the back bathroom at Crow Bar. They say love at first sight isn't real, but girl, that G string—"

"Oh, my GOD!"

"Bail, Gwen! Bail!"

"Dare I try a third?"

"Well, you know the number-one rule in this car."

"We must satisfy our insatiable curiosity?"

"Exactly."

"All right . . . Okay, this one."

"Rick, I love you, baby. Every song on—"

"Rick?"

"Yeah. Danny's bi. He's dating a guy named Tony right now. At least, I think they're still together."

"Maybe even moving in together?"

"Oh, shoot! I didn't think to ask. I've been a bad friend. I'll have to check in when I see him on Wednesday."

"Do we need to hear about whatever sexual encounter with Rick that Danny lovingly recounts before he plays him a song?"

"Perhaps we cede Danny his privacy and give up?"

"Fair enough. A shame though. There's gotta be like twenty tapes here. Do you think they're all love mixes?"

"Could be. I think the real question is whether or not all the songs are the same on each tape."

"He wouldn't! That didn't even occur to me."

"I mean, there's at least gotta be some repeats, right? If there are twenty tapes? Who could possibly know that many unique love songs that only reminded them of that one specific person?"

"Who could possibly have had twenty partners so meaningful to them they made a mix tape? Danny must have incredible stamina."

"Can we not talk about my childhood friend's stamina, please? I'm still trying to wipe the image of him and Jezebel surviving on nothing but body heat and love."

"Yes, there are truly some things that we're not supposed to know about our friends. That's why I'm so glad my roommate is moving out."

"Oh?"

"Yeah. We were pretty good friends before we started living together, but then she moved in and things have soured a bit. I'm hoping we'll rebound with a little space and time."

"What went wrong?"

"She's just very . . . free with her romantic life and I have seen and heard things that one is not supposed to see and hear. She's moving out to be with her partner and I am extremely relieved."

"Does . . . that mean you have a spare bedroom in your apartment?"

"Are you thinking about Paloma?"

"Well, no pressure, obviously. But I can certainly vouch for her. She's respectful and kind and I actually think you two would get along really well."

"Well, you can give her my phone number and we can chat and see if it's a fit. If I didn't have to venture to the blackhole of Craigslist roommates, I wouldn't be too mad about that. But I'll warn you, the apartment is really . . . not special. Mediocre views, mediocre amenities. I'm barely there, so once Fay takes all her things, I'm going to be left with . . . almost nothing. But, yeah, if you're still thinking Paloma would be interested, like I said, give her my number."

"Great! But, uh, actually *I* don't even have your number."

"Oh, right! That's so funny. We became friends so fast I didn't realize we'd skipped over a lot of the preliminaries. Can I see your phone? I'll put myself in."

"Here. It's unlocked."

"Oh. Who's this in your background picture with you?"

"Hm? Oh, that's Herman. He's one of my clients. Probably my favorite one, if I'm telling the truth."

"What medal is he holding up?"

"He'd just completed a half-marathon. I won't go into his medical history, but he and I have been working together for years, really hard. And the fact that he completed that race . . . I know I said that I've never won anything before, but watching Herman cross the finish line was an incredible feeling. I don't know if I've ever been prouder in my life. Of him or of me."

"His smile is, like, the purest thing I've ever seen."

"It was a really great moment. What's your phone background?"

"Oh. My cat. Garpy."

". . ."

"What's that look for?"

"I'm . . . just taking a minute with this information."

"The fact that I have a cat? It's that hard to understand?"

"Well, first of all, I thought for sure you'd say that your background picture was, like, you at some peak in the Andes or drinking wine on a riviera."

"Oh, come on."

"So, it was a shock that your background is something as quaint as your cat. Which, how do you take care of it when you're traveling? Also, I was taking a minute to deal with the fact that your cat's name is Garpy."

"I got him at a shelter near my parents' house and my niece was with me, so I let her name him. Garpy is a nickname for his full name, which is actually Garlic Pickle."

"You let your niece name your cat Garlic Pickle?"

"It's a solid name! They're not always the most attractive thing on the plate, but everybody loves a garlic pickle. It was apt. And my friend Carl already has two cats, so Garpy joins Carl's brood when I travel. It works for all of us."

"Wow. Gwen and Garpy. Garpy and Gwen. Imagine that."

"Okay. Now I'm officially in your phone and I'm calling my line from yours so . . . yup. I have your number too. What should I save you as?"

"I assume, since you asked, that saving me as Sam Champion is off the table?"

"Come on, we can be more creative than that."

"What did you save yourself as in my phone?"

"You'll find out later when you stop driving and check it out."

"Ahhhh. The insatiable curiosity is killing me. That's just cruel."

"How about I save you as . . . Bus Boy."

"Oh. Great. Just add the word 'adorable' in there and then my persona will be complete."

"Still hung up on that, huh?"

"Need I remind you what that teenager said about me? That I'm an M-A-N?"

"You'd rather be Bus *Man* in my phone?"

"Why do I have to be Bus anything?"

"Come on, it's a major aspect of your personality. Your affinity for discount bus rides."

"How about the fact that I have blue hair? That doesn't define me in your eyes?"

"You've already admitted that not only is the blue hair out of character, it's likely temporary. Hey, I just realized that your childhood friend saw you with blue hair for the first time in his life and didn't even bat an eye."

"He texted me about it while you were buying the taco salads."

"What'd he say?"

"Ah, uh, nothing."

"Come on . . ."

"He just said that he liked the hair and that you must be a good influence on me."

"Oh, he thought that *I* was the reason for the blue hair?"

"I guess so."

"Huh. What about me says blue hair enthusiast?"

"Uh, Gwen? Are you forgetting about the fact that you're wearing a girl tux on a random Sunday afternoon? I think you might seem a little *quirky* to the casual observer right now."

"Ah. Yes. Of course. I'm the quirky waif who is slowly convincing you to live a more whimsical life, free of social boundaries."

"I've seen that movie before. I think there's a lot of indie rock on the soundtrack."

"I bet some of those songs are buried somewhere on Danny's love mixes."

"Well, instead of you being a quirky waif, maybe I'm the dependable sheepdog type who is slowly romancing you into a more conventional lifestyle."

"Bor-ing."

"Totally. I'll be the waif. You be the sheepdog."

"That'll show 'em."

"How do you think Garpy will feel about his owner being a sheepdog?"

"What is it with you and Garpy? You're obsessed."

"It's just this totally unexpected detail about you. I like it."

"Okay. Well, give me an unexpected detail about you."

"Oh . . . unexpected, unexpected, unexpected . . . Um . . ."

"Are you freezing up like when you have to come up with topics?"

"Yes. Brain hurts."

"Okay, we'll come back to that. Instead . . . let's talk about . . . your apartment! What's your place like?"

"My place? Small. Like I said, it's a studio. But it's nice. I'm pretty fastidious."

"Do you have pillows on your couch?"

"Huh? Random question."

"I've found you can tell a lot about a person by what type of pillows, or not, they keep on their couch. So. Do you?"

"Yeah, actually. My aunt Laura cross-stitches famous paintings so there's one of *Starry Night* and one of Monet's *Water Lilies*."

"She likes the Impressionists."

"Yup. What do my pillows say about me in your estimation?"

"Mmm. Well, family man, obviously. And considering which paintings those are, you're not afraid of color in your space. And since your aunt painstakingly made them for you, you're probably not eating pizza slices with nothing but a napkin on your couch. And . . . this is more of a guess than anything but if you have these nice, handcrafted pillows, I bet your couch isn't flea-bitten, dragged in from the curb. I bet it's something nice. Probably something you had to save a little money to buy."

". . ."

"What?"

"I'm . . . afraid to say anything else."

"Why?"

"Because your extrapolation skills are unreal."

"I take it I was mostly right in my couch pillow analysis?"

"That was freaky. You really know your stuff."

"I'm telling you, Sam. I've interviewed hundreds of people about their lives and their aesthetic choices. I pay attention."

"Apparently."

"Okay . . . so, more about your apartment. You said you're fastidious. So, at this very second, is your bed made?"

"Always."

"And your nightstand?"

"Um. What about it?"

"What's on it right now?"

"Oh. Okay. You want to know what's *on* it. I thought you were asking what was, um, in it. But yeah. Never mind. Um. There's a stained-glass lamp and an alarm clock and my Kindle. Because I forgot to bring it to my mom's house."

"An alarm clock? Not your phone?"

"No. I don't like to keep my phone by my bed. Do you keep your phone beside your bed?"

"Of course. With the amount I travel, my phone is my lifeline. I feel super-nervous if I'm not able to reach it at night. Okay, how about your fridge? Exactly how much expired food is in your fridge right this very second? Don't think, just answer!"

"There's some slightly questionable Indian food from last week that I'll probably throw out when I get home. But other than that, I think everything is good."

"Hm."

"You sound disappointed."

"Some people's dirtiest little secrets are growing green stuff in their fridges."

"You're rooting around for my dirtiest little secrets?"

"I'm actually assuming that your dirtiest little secrets are living inside the nightstand you really didn't want to tell me about, but I won't pry *too* much. Considering you're absolutely saving my ass right now and I'd like to show my gratitude."

"I wonder if I really *do* have any dirty little secrets. Not really, unfortunately. I might be more interesting if I did."

"You're plenty interesting."

"You know, I only know one other person who can do what you just did."

"What did I just do?"

"See right through me. Make all sorts of accurate assumptions based on peanuts."

"Oh? Who?"

"Brenda."

"Ahhhh. The ruthless Brenda. Who is probably finding out my social security number right this very second. I hope she doesn't find out about that night in jail."

"I . . . actually think that you and Brenda would get along."

"You sound surprised by that realization."

"I mean . . . you're not the type of person my mother *thinks* she'd get along with."

"Nice Catholic girl from Scituate with dreams of settling down on her block and producing grandchildren?"

"Right. So, at the outset it seems like your relationship with her would be doomed. But . . . now that I think about it, personality-wise, I think you might be two peas."

"How so?"

"Well, my mother loves her hometown, and definitely doesn't want to live anywhere else, but I wouldn't call her a homebody. She's super-active. She's in about a hundred different clubs. And loves sports."

"What kind of sports?"

"Hiking and fishing and kayaking and stuff like that. She'll occasionally play pickleball with some of the other people on our cul-de-sac. But she's very outdoorsy. Stargazing and beach walks and all that sort of thing. She loves talking to people. But she also loves being alone with her thoughts.

She's also very politically active. She's been arrested before at protests."

"Wow, this is very different than how I was picturing her."

"You were picturing someone who timidly stays at home and depends on her son for literally everything? That I was her only connection to the world and she uses me for a stand-in for all her social needs?"

"Kind of?"

"Well, there have been times when that was true. And she's a little bit in that phase right now, because of how bad the break-up was. And she definitely leans on me. But she's a pretty dynamic person."

"It's kind of surprising to me that she's only had one relationship since your dad. She sounds like she'd be meeting people left and right."

"I think my dad was kind of . . . *it* for her. It took forever for her to do things like move his slippers away from his side of the bed."

"Oh, that's heartbreaking."

"I know . . . You know, I think she had a lot of people interested in her. But she just didn't see it, or want it, I'm not sure. Or she wasn't ready."

"Is she interested in travel?"

"I . . . I don't know, actually."

"I mean, I don't know how you would feel about it, but if you're getting a little antsy with spending all your vacation days in your hometown, is there any way that inviting your mom to do something somewhere else would be fun?"

"Traveling with my mother . . . I mean, maybe? I'd have to consider it. It's not something she and I have ever really talked about before."

"There's so many places you could go. Things to do. I could help plan a trip that's not so travel-hard, if you think she wouldn't like that. For instance, you can get to Iceland on less than a five-hour plane ride from NYC. And if she's into hiking and stargazing? Come on, that's the *dream* vacation spot right there. Icebergs. Glaciers. Volcanoes. Whale-watching. Northern lights. Hot springs. You name it. And the people are very friendly to tourists."

"You're so excited right now."

"Sorry."

"Don't be sorry. It's very cute. Your cheeks got all rosy. Your eyes lit up."

"Well, I obviously love talking about travel. And I loved my time in Iceland. Just talking about it makes me want to go back."

"You should come with us."

". . . With you and your mother?"

"Sorry. Is that weird? Sorry. Forget I said that. I just . . . said it. I don't know."

"So . . . you're serious that your mother would like me? I thought you were just gassing me up."

"The real truth is that my mother likes anyone who is good for me."

". . ."

". . ."

". . . And you think I'm good for you?"

"I mean . . . Don't you think *I'm* good for *you*?"

"Well, like I said, you're going well out of your way to save my tookus. So . . . yeah. Obviously. But what have I done for you?"

"You got me out of my turtle shell."

"Oh, because you never usually talk to your seatmates?"

"Yeah. You got me to finally meet Shirley. I hadn't talked to Danny in way too long. And, honestly, if I had to guess, you're going to get a homemade pie in the mail one of these days. He makes killer pies. They're not much to look at, but his flavors are unreal."

"Why is Danny gonna send me a pie?"

". . ."

"Ahhh. Because I finally got you to call in this mysterious favor that's been hanging over his head since . . . childhood? Teenagerhood?"

". . ."

"Is it super-embarrassing? This favor?"

"No. It's not, but it's embarrassing that he views it as a favor. Something to pay back. In my mind, it was just . . . what you do, if you can. And . . . but I get why it's weighed on him. Like a debt. He seemed so relieved to be able to do this for me. Maybe I should've come up with some way for him to 'repay' me a lot earlier. I don't think I realized how heavy this was for him."

"Sam?"

"Are you dying of insatiable curiosity?"

"*Dying.*"

"All right. I just . . . I always feel awkward when I talk about this because it feels like I'm bragging. But I don't mean to, and . . . oh fine, I'll just spit it out. When we were about fifteen, I donated bone marrow to his little sister. Who had leukemia at the time. She's since made a full recovery."

"*Wow.*"

"It's not even guaranteed that your family will be a match, but Danny and his sister are both adopted. So they couldn't find any close genetic matches to her. A bunch of us, his friends, I mean, took the test to see if we'd match with her and I was the only one. My mom was really freaked out because you have to go under general anesthesia, but she ultimately understood why I wanted to do it."

"You had the chance to help someone with cancer."

"*Exactly.* Wow, you understood that right away, huh? Even

though I was so young when my dad passed, I still remember just feeling totally helpless watching him deteriorate. I felt like there was nothing I could do. My mom felt that way too. So . . . when the opportunity came along to help Liz . . . I really wanted to do it. I think that's part of the reason why it's always felt weird to me that Danny felt like it was such a big favor. Because in a way it was a favor to me as well. I had this moment of intense action where I could put things right for her. For his whole family. And . . . of course . . . I was, am, really proud of myself. It was painful. And scary. But the impact it made . . . That's something I get to carry with me for my whole life. Not many people get that kind of gift. I . . . feel like a good person. And that is . . ."

"So rare."

"I think so. But anyways, I never wanted Danny to feel in debt to me over something that was so good for me too."

"He seemed so stoked to be able to return the favor."

"Yeah. Like I said, maybe I should have come up with something a long time ago just to let him let it go."

"Oh! Sam! Look! There's a flea market at this exit."

"Uh huh?"

"Let's stop."

"What?!"

"Look, we made up a bunch of time. Maps says that we're gonna be there with almost an hour to spare. Let's take fifteen minutes and stop at the flea."

"You want to stop at a flea market *now*? But what about Niles Shaw?"

"I checked at the gas station and he updated his social media from the air. By my calculation, he won't make it to Florine's with more than twenty minutes to spare. We have time! Besides. I *love* flea markets. They're the thing I love the most in this world. I always find something amazing and rare and . . . I feel like I really need a good luck charm right now. For the interview."

"Oh. Uh. Okay. If you say so. I guess we could probably give up about fifteen or twenty minutes."

"I'll change into my interview outfit so that we don't have to find a place to do that in the city. Two birds, one stone."

"Okay. Sure. Here we go."

Chapter Ten

Gwen

We get to the parking lot of the flea market and I practically explode out of the car. I'm sure he's expecting me to wander around with him in there. But I need a break from Sam.

There's not enough air in that car.

Did I say I needed to find a good luck charm?

It's more like a talisman.

Because I already have a good luck man. And now I need some sort of magic wand that'll ward off this feeling for him.

I'm so thirsty for him I could scream. Seriously. I want to put him over ice and swallow him down in two big gulps. I want a whipped cream mustache when I'm done. I want to lick him off the rim of the glass.

Which is a problem because Sam was a charming little distraction when he was just a cutie on a bus somehow beguiling me into talking about my life. I mean . . . it was unusual, but he was right. What did I have to lose?

But then . . . we exchange phone numbers. So that one of his best friends could potentially live with me. And then he invites me to Iceland? Sure, he took it back when he realized that it was making me freak out. But . . . that's the kind of person he is. He's someone who needs a core group of people, he says. And I'm someone who wouldn't know a core group of people if they hid behind my shower curtain.

In a matter of hours he's gone from flirty distraction to . . . to . . .

Look, I have never, ever, been a sucker for someone's stats before. But come on. This man is a scrupulous, practical-minded homemaker, who listed an old man's half-marathon win as one of the biggest accomplishments of his own life. He's respectful to his mother, he goes out of his way to help others, he has great relationships with female and queer friends. And now I find out he was a bone marrow donor and he's secretly proud of himself about it but he doesn't want to brag?

Come on, Cupid. Forget the arrows. Just use the machete and chop my head off already. I'm done. D-O-N-E.

He is the opposite of anyone I've ever dated and he is completely wrong for me and all I can think about is whatever horrid break-up text I'd have to send him sometime in the next calendar year.

Having a crush on Sam is fine. Doing anything about my crush on Sam makes absolutely no sense at all considering that man out there is the last person on earth I'd ever want to see with a broken heart. Let alone a broken heart courtesy of yours truly.

Also . . . he's making me very gabby. About things that I didn't even know I wanted to gab about.

I burst through the doors of the indoor flea market and that familiar smell swamps me. Cedar, slight mold, old books, potpourri, French fries, yeasty beer. Ahhh. Yes. Soothe me.

I hear him shout my name from behind me and I turn and point to my bag and then the bathrooms to let him know that I'm going to change my clothes first.

I need time.

Because I've still got some time locked in a car with this

man and I'm not sure if I'm going to get out of this without telling him about the whole whipped cream idea.

I have never, ever, been good at keeping a crush a secret.

It's not my natural inclination, and honestly, I never really saw the point. If you like someone, of course you have to tell them, otherwise they might never know and then nothing will ever happen with them.

But see? He's about to go on a date with someone for whom he's carried a torch for a decade. And I'm hopefully about to make enough money to be able to catapult myself into another hemisphere for the foreseeable future. Which is exactly what I want.

In order for this logic to work, I have to ignore the fact that Sam is also what I want. But you can't have everything you want!

Plus, we've only known one another for, like, a single afternoon.

I'm aware that the outlook isn't great on this one.

I lock myself into one of the stalls and pull out my most interview-ready outfit and, thank goodness, it hasn't wrinkled too badly. Unlike my poor tux that sadly looks as if I wore it into a sauna and then slept on a bench for a night or two. I change my clothes in the stall and when I emerge, I catch sight of myself in the mirror and for a moment, I'm shocked.

Because I've just transformed from Bus Tux Girl to Gwen Cellar, photographer and writer, here to interview one of the most famous recluses in the history of Manhattan socialites. Not to mention she's a killer photographer herself. And, oh yeah, one of my heroes. And I . . . have not prepared for this interview at all.

The thing is, I don't really prepare for *any* of my interviews. I've gotten good at winging them, and for the most part, they're better if they're more off the cuff and less rehearsed. The conversation flows better and people tend to get more comfortable with me than if I'm clacking papers into piles and pausing to refer to notes.

But this isn't any old interview.

I'm lucky that I've always admired her so much because when my editor first came up with this as a potentiality, I wasn't working from scratch. So, I'm not at square one. But still, I've spent the last half a day flirting with a lanky blue-haired man instead of preparing.

Meanwhile, I can practically feel Niles Shaw cracking his knuckles somewhere over Minnesota, internet-sleuthing his way into finding out Florine Weatherbell's favorite muffin or some such crap he thinks will give him the edge.

I need . . . to center myself. I need to *focus*. I've already decided two important things here. One: I like Sam. And two: There's no way anything is ever gonna come of it. So, when we get back into that car, I'm going to stop flirting and get down to business.

I brush my teeth, put on a few touches of makeup, brush my straight hair out and braid a bit of it back so that it doesn't hang into my eyes.

Transformation complete, I leave the restroom and walk back out into the big warehouse-style market. It's not too crowded, but for a moment, I wonder how I'll ever find Sam in all the square footage.

But then I see it, his stripe of indigo, burning under the hanging lights, calling me to him. Blue, what a taste. Blueberry, blackberry, sour-sweet swallows of the most intense flavors. I'm so thirsty.

He sees me coming and looks up. He blinks. And blinks. And blinks. By the time I get to him, he's gone quite pink in the cheek. Pink cheeks, dark green eyes, blue and brown hair. Heck of a color palette.

As I wonder how the hell I'm going to get through the rest of this afternoon, he clears his throat and starts to jabber.

"Uh. Ah. I've been out here scouting out some potential lucky charms."

"Huh?"

"There are some quill pens with feathers on the ends over there. I thought that might be a good good luck charm, because, you know, you're a writer. And then there are these charm bracelets over in this direction. I don't know much about charm bracelets, but they have the word 'charm' in their name, so I thought that might be a good bet for a good luck charm. But then, if you wanted something really simple, there are these buckets of marbles to choose from right over here."

"Oooooo. Wow, look at them all together in the light like that. They're so beautiful. Like a bucket full of gems."

"Yeah. It's kind of magical. And they're really cheap."

"I think you found it. I'll choose one of these. Or . . . better yet, you choose one for me."

"You want me to choose your lucky charm? Shouldn't you be the one to choose it? Hold it in your hand and wait for it to speak to you or something?"

"That is . . . a very romantic idea. Much more whimsical than I'd have given you credit for. Maybe you really are the quirky waif and I'm the staid sheepdog."

"You're the one who wanted to come into a flea market to find a good luck charm!"

"That was mostly an excuse."

"For what?"

"Are you gonna choose me a marble or not? Here, I'll choose one for you too. That way we'll be even. Mmmmm. This one. For you."

"What made you pick this one?"

"It's transparent. Hiding no secrets. What you see is what

you get. But a light green color, like it's a little bit shy, not quite bold. But then, there at the bottom, a little squiggle of yellow. It's changing its stripes little by little."

"Wow. That is . . . you can really analyze on your feet."

"Is that one for me?"

"Oh. Yeah. I don't have . . . I can't do the whole metaphor deep-dive the way you just did. But it's . . . pretty. Like you. And the swirly parts are like flower petals. And I probably don't have time to get you flowers on your big day today, so this'll have to do."

"And the swirly parts are indigo blue. Same color as your hair."

"Oh. God. I didn't notice that. That's so embarrassing. Here, give it back. I'll choose another. That's not why I—"

"No! Never. I'm not giving it back. I love this one. It's perfect. I held it in my hand and it sang to me just like you said it would. Sir, here's fifty cents for these two marbles. Thank you! Okay, Sam, let's blow this pop stand."

"Do you think anyone has ever actually done that? Blown a pop stand on their way out of town?"

"The saying had to come from somewhere. What's this for?"

"It's twenty-five cents. For the marble. You paid for both. Come on, you can't buy your own good luck charm. The whole point was buying them for each other."

"Hey, Sam?"

"Mmhmm?"

"When we get back to the car, I'm going to have to prep for my interview a little bit."

"Oh! Of course. Gosh, why didn't I think of that before. I'm sorry, have I been keeping you from your work?"

"No. Not at all. If anything you've been keeping me loose, which is way better than being anxious all day. But, yeah, while I was changing, I was trying to shift my brain to the interview and so . . . I think I need to *actually* shift my brain to the interview."

"No problem at all. I'll be so quiet. Like a chauffeur."

"We can listen to the radio or something."

"No, no. I'm fine with the quiet. You just work away. I'll focus on getting us there in one piece."

Chapter Eleven

Sam

Gwen has been alternately scratching away at a notebook and gazing out the window for twenty minutes now. I'm trying not to look over at her too often because she is clearly deep in thought.

But . . . it's hard not to look over at her too often because she is so pretty my hands are sweating on the steering wheel.

Have you ever had a movie soundtrack moment? Where for one second it becomes very clear that your life *must* be on someone else's TV screen because there's a moment so choreographed, so perfect, it must have been written by some writer-god? And you're just certain that the perfect song must be playing in the background somewhere? Like how when 'I Wanna Dance With Somebody' plays at a party and, even if no one is dancing yet, everybody automatically gets up and dances? There's an automatic dance scene and it becomes clear that there is some sort of narrative plan for all of us and we're all just bopping along in our lives, able to get swept up in it at a moment's notice?

Yeah, well, perhaps the semi-sensical ramblings here should be an indicator that one of those moments just happened to me and it just about knocked me sideways.

Picture this: you're in a totally random flea market in Connecticut looking at a very strange set of snow globes (you're almost certain that one of them is displaying Blackbeard snoozing under a palm tree . . . in the snow) while a grumpy man barks at you, "No touching" and you've just started wondering about the many curious smells you're currently being subjected to when, for some reason, you straighten up and turn to look over your shoulder.

And there she is.

Here's the thing about a crush. There are a lot of different kinds. Some of them are happy to pleasantly pluck away at a harp or an acoustic guitar in the corner of your mind. Some of them tap at the mic and ask for center stage. And some of them . . . some of them fly-tackle you and shove snow down your pants.

Guess which one Gwen is for me.

The crowd parted—somewhere for some cosmic audience, I'm sure the perfect song dropped in the background—and for me, I just stopped breathing while she walked over to me. Brushed and polished and smiling. She's got such a great smile.

All I could think?

Thank you, peanut butter sandwich.

Thank you for making me miss my neighbor's ride into the city this morning. Thank you, city buses, for being ten minutes behind schedule. Thank you, every other passenger who didn't want to sit across from the bus bathroom. Thank you for leaving one last seat and having it be next to Gwen.

Because if everything had gone as usual, I would have been sitting at the front of the bus with my headphones in and might never even have seen her.

But instead, all thanks to that perfect, wonderful, irritating peanut butter sandwich, instead, I got to be the guy, the one guy, she walked across a flea market to smile at.

And now I get to be the guy, the one guy, who drives her into Manhattan for her big interview . . .

. . . where I will leave her and then race down to the bus stop in hopes of not doing the rudest thing ever and standing Katie McConnick up.

My mother must be stopped. What a menace.

I texted her twice more in the flea market, asking for Katie's number, but she refused to give it to me. When I called her she didn't answer. She knows something is afoot and won't give me the chance to cancel the date properly. Thus compelling me to attend said date.

Though we're still a bit over an hour out according to maps, as the crow flies we're getting pretty close to the Bronx and I merge from the speedy, wide-open expressway onto the two-lane parkway where the traffic slows and the trees crowd out the sky.

Every mile we get closer to the city I get simultaneously more relaxed and more tense. I'm not usually someone who gets too bogged down in superstitions, but Gwen's marble is pressed against my leg in my pocket and the little yellow spray at the bottom is almost burning me. "*Not quite bold . . . but it's changing its stripes little by little*," she said. And I've never wanted to change my stripes more than right now.

I know that she doesn't want Niles Shaw. The idea that he could steal from her professional portfolio and then still believe that he might be able to date her is so repulsively arrogant it makes me want to tear a pillow in half, so I can only imagine how it makes Gwen feel. But I was serious when I asked her if the life Niles Shaw lives makes him the kind of guy she imagines herself with.

The truth is, no matter how far I let my imagination wander, that is not me. It'll never be me. Money, mom, responsibility, these are core tenets to who I am. And if I were tempted to change that about myself for a woman, I should be skeptical of that attraction because it's probably not healthy.

But, but, but . . . I've never borrowed a car to race someone somewhere. I've never been a save-the-day kind of guy before. And maybe . . . maybe that's the yellow at the bottom of the marble. Maybe trying my absolute hardest to dropkick fate out of Gwen's way and get her to the Upper East Side in time is changing my stripes. Maybe . . . booking an unexpected vacation is changing my stripes. Maybe bailing on a date I didn't want my mother to set up is changing my stripes. No. No, I can't stand up Katie, because that's just rude and I wouldn't want Katie to be collateral damage to all this stripe-changing I'm attempting to do at warp speed.

But still, these are tangible, reachable goals.

Big white mustache? Drinking brandy from my personal balcony overlooking the Eiffel Tower? Not reachable.

Getting Gwen to Florine Weatherbell's if it kills me? Possible.

My phone buzzes in my pocket and I just know it's my mother. I also know what it's going to be. More bits and pieces of information she's gleaned about Gwen. I know because she texted me while I was in the flea market.

Yes, that's right. She's completely ignored my requests for Katie's number and, instead, texted me two different articles that Gwen has written for her friend's magazine. My mother offered no commentary on these articles, so I have no idea what she thought about them. She just passed them along to me as . . . I don't know? Just a little background information on the woman she thinks I'm still sitting next to on the bus?

I wonder what would happen if I told my mother the bus broke down and I'm driving Gwen in Danny's car. I bet *that* would get her on the horn.

But is that a conversation I'd be willing to have with Gwen in the passenger seat? Um. Short answer, no.

I can see why Gwen was so surprised when I described my mother's personality. Because on the one hand, she'd seem like a total busy-body nag who wants nothing more than to control every aspect of her son's life. Thus painting *me* as the completely malleable mama's boy who never learned to stand up for himself and is thus destined to let his mother lick her finger and smooth his eyebrows down for life.

Please believe me when I say that that is not me.

She's just complicated. And lost right now. And, not to sound self-centered, but I am definitely my mother's true north. If I can give her a little direction, let her fuss over having—quote unquote—"destroyed my beautiful head of hair" and let her set me up on a date or two, then . . . I guess I've come to view that as the same sort of mental exercise for her as a sudoku puzzle. It gives her brain something to do for a while so that she's not hamster-wheeling over her break-up. Soon enough, she'll be over it and back to her clubs and active lifestyle and I'll be off the hook and back to my own regularly scheduled programming.

The weird part is that besides the inflexible timing and the total surprise factor, this Katie McConnick debacle isn't the worst blind-date scenario from her. In a different world, my mother setting me up with someone I used to have a crush on in high school is, admittedly, better odds at chemistry and connection than her setting me up with total strangers who happen to meet her standards. But, over the course of this afternoon it has become increasingly clearer to me that I should *not* be going on a blind date with anyone right now. Because I would very much like to go on a regular date with the woman in the passenger seat of this car.

"Gwen, do you think the term 'blind date' is ableist?"

"Huh?"

"Oh! Sorry. I was thinking out loud. I didn't mean to

interrupt. I just had a thought and then . . . talked it. My bad. Get back to prepping. I'll be quiet."

"No, it's okay. I actually got a lot done just now. I feel pretty good about the interview. And . . . that's a very good question. And, I'm gonna go with 'yes', I think it's probably ableist. Think about it, it doesn't even really describe the situation accurately."

"Right. It really just means a date with someone you don't know yet. And maybe don't even know what they look like."

"Exactly, why bring blind people into it?"

"So what should we call that kind of date instead?"

"How about . . . newbie date?"

"Oh, that's good. Novice date?"

"I like it. I like it. . . . Fledgling date?"

"Oh, that's perfect. Because your relationship is like a little baby bird that might never make it into flight. Okay, perfect. Vocab officially switched. Fledgling date it is."

"I mean, no one will likely know what you're talking about when you use that term, but . . ."

"That's okay. I'll just explain it. And, to be honest, I kind of hope I don't have a lot of reason for referencing that kind of date very much in the future."

"Oh. Ah . . . high hopes for you and Katie, huh?"

"Huh? Oh—"

"Is that what made you wonder that term? Thinking about your date?"

"Sort of. But mostly . . . as a physical therapist, I think a lot about ableism because unfortunately a lot of my clients have to deal with it in various forms. It's one of those things that even well-meaning people sort of unconsciously do. Like using the term 'blind date' and not realizing that it could diminish the experiences of a blind person. So . . . yeah. I try to think about it. Work in progress, I guess."

"Ugh."

"Ugh what?"

"You're just . . . you're a really good person."

"Oh. You sound . . . thrilled about that."

"You're probably, like, a really great friend, right?"

"Are you profiling me again? Like when you thought I was a lazy boyfriend?"

"No, it's just a guess. But you probably remember birthdays and show up with flowers when your friends defend their dissertations or something like that? I want a friend like that. I don't want to just . . . lose that."

"Hold on. We are friends. We already decided that, right? Did I miss something?"

"No . . . it's just that . . . I'd really like to . . . But, look, Sam. I'm in and out of the city so much. You're gonna get sick of my schedule at some point. And I just . . . Can I make a request?"

"Sure?"

"Can you just . . . be a normal, regular old nothing-special guy for the next hour or so?"

"What?"

"Just . . . don't . . . knock any socks off. Of anybody, okay? Just be, like, boring or something. I have this big interview. You have this big date. And I think . . . everything would be easier if we just . . . underwhelmed each other. Don't you think?"

"I'm sorry, what?"

"Underwhelm me."

"You want me to . . ."

"Really alter my expectations of you, all right? I'm not saying do anything *cruel*. Just . . . be, like, an average guy with, like, masculinity issues and weirdly porny expectations for your girlfriends. Just, like, mildly disappoint me for a little while, okay?"

"You would prefer if I were mildly disappointing?"

"Like I said, at least until we get there. It would really help me out."

"I . . . you . . . I . . . but . . ."

"You seem confused."

"There are a *lot* of lines to read between right now, Gwen."

"There are no lines. Just come on. Say something disappointing. You squeeze the toothpaste from the top? You, magically, are only attracted to perfect tens? You think ghosting is an appropriate way to dump someone! Disenchant me a little!"

"And this . . . will help you get in the right mind space for your interview?"

"Yeah. I need both feet on the ground. It's weird to have met such a good guy randomly. It's throwing me off. Dump a bucket of ice water over my head or something."

"Okay . . . um . . . dogs are the worst."

"What?!"

"Yeah. I really can't stand them. They're so silly—I'm sorry, I can't do it. Dogs are God's gift to humans. We barely deserve them. Let me try a different tactic. Um . . . okay, learning a different language is a waste of time!"

"Oh, boy."

"Yeah, um, everyone in the world should learn English. Uh . . . All the other languages are, uh, pointless. They have no value and—seriously, why am I doing this? I feel like I'm bringing bad karma down on my head or something. You know I don't really feel that way, don't you? Learning other languages is obviously super rad. And important. And—"

"Sam."

"Yeah?"

"You're really bad at this."

"Disappointing you?"

"Yeah."

"Isn't that a good thing?"

"Let's . . . just . . . change the subject. Oh, your phone is buzzing anyway."

"Oh. Yeah. Can you check it? I'm sure it's my mom and I was trying to get ahold of her in the flea market. Fair warning, it's likely another one of the articles you wrote for your friend's magazine. She's already sent me two of them."

"For real?"

"Oh, yeah."

"Did she say anything about them?"

"Nope. Just passing them along to me."

"In . . . like . . . a judgy way?"

"No, I don't think so. I think she's just . . . a boomer. And thinks that she needs to text me things like that about my friends."

"Ah. Huh. Well, like I said, I really don't text with my parents so maybe your mom's behavior is perfectly within the range of normal?"

"Well, normal or not, I'm certainly *used* to it. Was that text from her?"

"Oh. Yeah, it's her. I can't read it though, your phone is locked."

"Here, take my thumb, will you unlock it for me?"

"No one's ever told me to take their thumb before. What a time we live in. There you go."

"Oh. It's just a picture. All blurry. I can't even see it. Can you tell what that is?"

". . ."

"Gwen?"

"It's a picture of a picture. I think she found an old photo and texted you a picture of it. It's a group shot. Oh, my God. This must be you in high school."

"Wait, really? Don't look! It's going to be humiliating."

"For *you*."

"Yes, exactly. Humiliating for *me*."

"And so fun for me!"

"Nooooooo. Exit out. Exit out."

"Are you kidding me? You're so cuuuuuuute. Like, nine feet tall compared to everyone else."

"I had an early growth spurt."

"And your smile."

"Yes. It's likely very sparkly from all the orthodontia."

"Oh, she just texted a caption. It says 'the only picture I could find of . . . you and Katie'."

"Oh."

"So, uh, Katie's in this picture too, huh? Which one is she?"

"I don't wanna look while I'm driving."

"There are only two girls in the photo. Redhead or brunette?"

"Brunette."

"Ah. Found her. She's right next to you. Very cute. I wonder what she looks like nowadays."

"I have no idea."

"You really never looked her up on Facebook or IG or something?"

"No. I don't spend a lot of time online. And besides, something about that just seemed a little too . . . It was just a high-school crush, you know? Not a love story for the ages. I knew that there was no reason to hang on to her from a distance if I hadn't even been able to muster up the courage to ask her out, you know?"

"Huh. Well . . . I guess you'll get the chance to rectify all that this evening."

". . ."

". . ."

"Hey, Gwen?"

"Mmhmm?"

"What if . . . what if I—"

"—Hey, do you wanna see a picture of *me* in high school? Eye for an eye?"

"Huh? Oh. Yes. Absolutely. One hundred percent. Immediately."

"Okay . . . let me find one. I should have at least one in my camera roll."

"Wanna do the camera roulette game?"

"What's that?"

"It's where one person scrolls through their camera roll at random and wherever their thumb lands, they have to show that picture to the other person."

"This . . . sounds like a drinking game."

"It is. Paloma and Vera and I play it sometimes. If you don't want to show the picture, the only way you can get out of it is to drink. And if the person you show the picture to screams or has a huge reaction *they* have to drink."

"Who made up this game?"

"I can't remember but I'm thinking it was probably Vera. She can make anything fun. You'll get it when you meet her."

". . ."

"Did I say something wrong?"

"No. Not at all. It's just . . . you want me to meet your friends."

"Oh. Of course. I mean, if you want to. You've already met Danny. Vera and Paloma are a piece of cake compared to him."

"Okay. So. Camera roulette?"

"You're in?"

"Should I close my eyes? Doesn't matter. I answered my own question. Here I go, and . . . Oh, boy."

"What?"

"We are . . . starting out intensely."

"What's the picture of?"

"Wait. What's my penalty if I don't want to show it to you? I'm obviously not going to drink right now."

"I bet Danny has some kind of moonshine in the back."

"You're encouraging me to drink immediately before my big interview? Sam Champion, you're such a bad influence! I should have known it when I saw your blue hair and leather jacket."

"I . . . have never worn a leather jacket in my life."

"Your motorcycle, then."

"Don't say motorcycle to me. It's like Betelgeuse. My mother will hear the word from three states away and teleport to this car and kick my ass just for talking about one."

"I guess you're officially not a bad influence, then."

"Yeah. No drinking. How about . . . truth or dare, then? That's the penalty? For not showing the picture."

"Hmm. Very high school."

"Well, the heart and soul of this game is trading high school photos, no?"

"Fair enough. Okay. I accept the terms of camera roulette. And I'll choose . . . truth, I guess?"

"What? You're already refusing to show the camera roll?"

"Yup."

"At least tell me the nature of the photo you're not showing me. Heartbreaking? Boring? Scandalous?"

"Scandalous. Not for public consumption. Brenda would have me arrested for debauching you. Now, what's my truth?"

"Your truth . . . um. Okay . . . When was the last date you went on?"

"Maybe three or four months ago? Okay, your turn."

"That's it? Those are all the details you're going to give me?"

"Hey! You asked the question, I answered the question. I've played enough truth or dare in my life to know better than to give up the goods for free. Now, your turn. Oh. Crap. You're driving. You can't play camera roulette when you're driving!"

"How about I just take the penalty every time? Yeah?"

"Mmmm. Okay. But you owe me a slideshow at some point."

"Deal. I'll hook it up to my TV. You can get every embarrassing photo in full HD."

"Have you no shame?"

"Just trying to honor the sanctity of camera roulette."

"Okay. Truth or dare?"

"Ummm. Truth?"

"Has your mother ever liked anyone you've ever dated?"

"Um. Sort of?"

"Sort of?"

"Well . . . I've only introduced her to two girlfriends. One of them she really didn't like. The other one she sort of liked. But . . . the truth is, neither of those people liked *her* very much either. She's kind of . . . a tough nut to crack."

"Does she like Vera and Paloma?"

"Oh. Yeah. She likes them both a lot. Vera sent her a package just the other day to help cheer her up from the break-up. It meant a lot to her."

"And you think she'd like me."

"I do. Um. Eventually."

"That . . . sounds like an insult?"

"No. No, it's not, I swear. I guess . . . I guess I just think that you're not easily intimidated, right? And if someone doesn't automatically like you, you don't necessarily give up, right? So . . . I think that you have a personality type that would eventually win my mother over. Regardless of whatever bad first impression she might make on you, I think you'd keep trying. What do you think? Is that just total bullshit?"

"Hmm."

"Hey! I just realized that you got, like, five answers from one turn! You fox!"

"You've gotta get in where you fit in, Sam. My turn? Okay, I'm scrolling and . . . Yeah. Truth, I guess."

"Another picture you're not showing me? How many scandalous photos do you have saved on your phone?"

"Nunya. Unless that's your official truth question. In which case you're going to have to be quiet while I count."

"No, no. What about your parents?"

"What about them?"

"Do they like any of your boyfriends?"

"Never introduced them to a single one."

"What? Are you serious?"

"As a heart attack."

"Have all your boyfriends been long distance or something?"

"You're picturing fictional Luc the sugar daddy right now, aren't you?"

"I mean . . . you're saying you've had local boyfriends and you still didn't introduce them ever?"

"My parents aren't interested in meeting boyfriends. They want to meet one single fiancé. And ideally, they'd have liked to have met him about eight years ago."

"Ah. I see. So, you haven't introduced any of your boyfriends in order to protect them from your parents?"

"Yes . . . and . . . wait! Your turn. Ask again later."

"Ahhh. Damn! I thought I had laid the breadcrumbs perfectly so you wouldn't notice."

"Alas."

"Yes. Alas. All right . . . instead of truth . . . how about a dare?"

"A dare? While you're driving?"

"Gotta be creative."

"Okay. I dare you to roll down the window and blow a kiss to that car that's about to pass us."

"Done . . . Here we go . . . *Mwah!* . . . Oh, my God."

"Sam, I think you made a friend!"

"I think I made more than a friend, did you see her face?"

"Man, you really did that with no reservations whatsoever, huh?"

"I handle truth or dare with the utmost seriousness. After all, it was responsible for my first kiss. And my second and third, now that I think about it."

"Ah. I get it now. I was wondering why you approached it with this level of reverence. It all makes sense now."

"Your turn."

"Right, right, scrolling . . . and . . . ah, this one I can actually show you."

"That is . . . a picture of the back of your head?"

"Yeah. I don't have a good mirror situation in my apartment so sometimes I take a picture of the back of my head to make sure my hair isn't a rat's nest back there. And then I forget to delete them."

"What a waste of a turn!"

"What?"

"I've seen the back of your head like a million times already! The point of camera roulette is to see shocking and appalling sides of your friends."

"You feel robbed? Oh, fine. You can truth or dare me."

"Excellent. Which is it?"

"Oh. Truth, I guess."

"Okay, what's the other reason you haven't brought any boyfriends to meet your parents? You said that you haven't introduced any boyfriends because you wanted to protect them from your parents and then you said 'and' like there was another reason. But then you trailed off and made me blow a kiss to that lovely octogenarian in the Lincoln."

". . ."

"Unless it's too personal?"

"No, no. I can share it with you . . . It's just that . . . ah, this is going to sound so ridiculous. But, people mean the word 'boyfriend' in a lot of different ways. Like, it can have this very serious ring to it, you know? You break your arm and your boyfriend shows up at the ER and the nurse is all, 'Who are you?' and he says, 'I'm her *boyfriend*.' Or at the office Christmas party when he puts an arm around your shoulders in front of your lecherous boss and says, 'Nice to meet you, I'm Julie's *boyfriend*.'"

"Lucky Julie."

"Right?"

"Are you coming up with these examples off the top of your head?"

"No. These are friends of mine."

"And these friends mean the word 'boyfriend' in very serious ways."

"Yes. In a life partner sort of way."

"But that's not how you generally mean it?"

"I think I've always kind of meant it in the most lighthearted way possible? Like . . . hey, guys, this is my boyfriend, AKA the guy who I'm dating for a while before I leave for three months and we date other people?"

"Ah."

"And who brings *that* kind of boyfriend home to their parents?"

"So, you've never been in a serious relationship?"

"I mean . . . I've been head over heels for someone before. And had really rough break-ups. But . . . if you bring someone home to your family . . . aren't you kind of implying that you would like that someone to someday be a *part* of your family?"

"I . . . guess? In the vaguest of terms."

"And I have just never felt that way before. About any of the someones."

"You've never dated someone who would show up at the ER if you broke your arm?"

"Sam, I wouldn't even call my *parents* to show up at the ER if I broke my arm."

". . ."

"Are you all right? What's that expression?"

"I just . . . hate that for you. Who's your In Case of Emergency?"

"I . . . don't really have a set one? It changes. It was my roommate for a while, but she's moving out, so . . . I don't know. Maybe I'll change it back to my sister. That'll be good motivation to never have any emergencies."

"What if you have to get dental surgery! What'll you do then?"

"Um."

"You have to call me if you get dental surgery, all right?"

"Sam."

"No, I'm serious. I had dental surgery a few years ago and the anesthesia knocked me on my *ass*. If I'd tried to get home on my own I would have ended up in, like, Nova Scotia or something. No, no. If you get dental surgery you need an In Case of Emergency. And not some random roommate who you don't really like, okay? Just call me and I'll make sure you get home safe. And have chicken soup. I actually make really great chicken soup. It's an old family recipe from my dad's mom. The trick is putting the celery in at the exact right moment . . . Feel free to cut me off at any time, okay?"

"I thought I'd let you run out of steam on your own."

"I almost passed out from oxygen loss."

"While driving, no less. Are you sure you're responsible enough to be my In Case of Emergency after hypothetical dental surgery?"

"It doesn't have to be me. But . . . I just don't like the idea of you toughing through stuff like that."

"You feel very passionately about chicken soup."

"I feel very passionately about people I care about not ending up in Nova Scotia."

"What's your beef with Nova Scotia?"

"Nothing. I'm sure it's lovely. Just not under the influence of laughing gas."

"Well, I promise I won't go to Nova Scotia under the influence of laughing gas."

"You're so . . ."

"I'm so . . ."

"You're just so . . ."

"I'm just so . . ."

"Confounding."

"Confounding?!"

"Yeah. I mean . . . you're ridiculously easy to talk to. Social and interesting and charismatic . . . but you don't have a proper In Case of Emergency."

"And this confounds you?"

"I just feel like I'm missing something."

"Missing something?"

"Yeah. I mean, everything you're saying implies that your family treats you like you're difficult. But . . . you're, like, *immediately* lovable. So, I don't get it. What's the missing piece?"

". . ."

"Oh. Crap. Sorry. That is just totally not my business, is it?

I'm sorry. Or, maybe I'm totally wrong, I don't know. Please forget I—"

"You're not totally wrong. At all."

". . ."

"Nobody has ever asked it quite like that, though."

"Sorry. Nosy. I think I come by it naturally. Brenda taught me well. Or poorly, depending on your point of view. Sorry."

"No, it's . . . actually kind of nice? I mean, you tell people you don't have a close relationship with your family and they just kind of say, okay. . . . So this is new."

"Well, I'm listening, if you wanted to say more."

". . ."

"Or not. That's totally fine too."

"You know, people don't usually just *ask* like that."

"Was it rude? It was totally rude, wasn't it? Sorry. It's something about you, I swear. No, not you. I'm not trying to blame it on you. But like I explained before, I'm usually the opposite of nosy. I do my best to suppress my inner Brenda. But with you? I don't know what it is. Chemistry or something. I've just been asking everything today."

"Ugh. This is totally the opposite of what I said I'd be doing right now."

"You should be prepping for the interview, you mean?"

"No. I . . . Oh, I give up. You're too . . . you. There's no fighting it. All right . . . Would everything you don't understand about me make more sense if I told you that my parents aren't my parents?"

"Oh. Really?"

"Yeah. I mean, I call them Mom and Dad. And I've been living with them since I was eight. But the person I call Mom is actually my biological aunt. I'm technically her niece. I'm her sister's daughter."

"Oh, wow."

"My biological mom died when I was really young. Wendy. And my biological dad was never in the picture. So, after Wendy passed away I went to my parents' family. They already had my sister. She's a bit younger than I am. So, I think it was a lot for them. All at once. To go from one kid to two. To suddenly have to figure out how to parent this kid who was so different from theirs. I know they love me. And things were easier when I lived there and we all just *had* to make do. But . . . my guess is that they just never quite got used to me? I don't know. I'm very different from them, like I said. And . . . I definitely make them nervous. I guess I'm a lot like my biological mom was. She wasn't a writer or a photographer. But she traveled all the time and never stayed in the same place for long. She was kind of hippy-ish, I guess. And she and my mom never understood one another very well. My parents never tried to change me, thank God, but they were never very comfortable with me, either. Like I said, I'm the oddball. I moved out after high school and we just stopped having things to talk about. They have no idea what to do with me. And the only news they'd ever want to hear is that I'm moving home to get a nine-to-five and marry a solid man. Everything else is just . . . a mystery to them."

"Oh, Gwen. Wow. That sounds so . . . Can I ask a question?"

"Sure."

"When you say that you're different from your family, you sound almost . . . like you're reminding yourself that it's true?"

"Really? I . . . I don't know. I don't have a lot of practice talking about this. I guess, since I moved out, we all understand one another through the ways that we're nothing alike. It's very simple this way. They're birds of a feather, and I'm . . . a traveling salesman."

"Hm."

"What's 'hm'?"

"Do you *like* being different from them?"

"It's not an issue of like or dislike, it just is the way it is. They're all like one another and I'm more like the way my bio mom was. My life has a certain rhythm to it, because that's the way it successfully operates. And theirs has a certain rhythm to it and our rhythms don't match. And if I ever tried to match them up I'd probably just . . . lose the beat? Sorry, that was corny. I just . . . do you get what I mean?"

"Sort of. It sounds very complicated."

"I know, I know, it's a lot . . . Let's . . . change the subject. Do you choose truth or dare?"

". . ."

"Come on. Truth or dare?"

"We don't *have* to change the subject, you know. I'll talk to you about this if you want. Or listen about this. You've listened all about my mom."

"Let's . . . take it easy. I've never broken it all down for someone before. At least, not someone I've only known since lunchtime."

"Fair enough. Thank you, though."

"For what?"

"Telling me."

"Blame it on our chemistry."

"But still. Chemistry notwithstanding, it means a lot to be let in to someone's life like that, and . . . Yeah. I don't take it lightly. So, thanks."

"Are you still stumping for my vote?"

"Huh?"

"You're running a pretty strong campaign to be my dental surgery In Case of Emergency."

"Ah. Yes. It's all politics in this car. You shouldn't trust a word I say."

"Unless it's under the umbrella of truth or dare. Which you treat with utter inviolability."

"It's all a means to an end. Don't forget you owe me a high school picture."

"Oh, right. Let me see if I can find one . . . In the meantime, talk about something else."

"Hmm. Topics. Topics. Topics."

"You said this weekend in particular was really difficult for your mom, right?"

"Oh. Yeah."

"Bad enough to dye your hair blue."

"Yeah . . ."

"What was so bad about it?"

"Well, you know, the break-up didn't happen that long ago. And it was totally out of the blue. Like, one day he just called her up and said he'd met someone new and he was crazy in love with her and things were over with my mom."

"Oof."

"Yeah. At first she kind of took it on the chin. She was mad more than anything. But then him and this new woman got engaged and their picture was in the lifestyle section of the paper and my mom happened to see it. And she realized that he'd proposed to this new woman with a ring that my mom had found about a year ago, thinking it was for her. So . . . then she got to thinking, *Was that ring really for me but he just didn't love me enough to give it to me? Was it always for her and he's been cheating for a long time?* Her anger kind of turned to confusion and she got really upset. And the wedding was like a high-speed train. Like, he's barely been broken up with my mom for two months and he and the new woman already got married this weekend. And it was this big, fancy deal. Like five hundred people. So, yeah, she really needed some distractions. Hence, the timing for my visit and my hair."

"He . . . got married this weekend?"

"Yeah."

"To someone he just met?"

"Maybe. Or maybe he'd known her longer. We don't really know. The worst part is that George and my mom were together for six or seven years, like I said. So they have a ton of the same friends. And the wedding was huge. So, like, everyone my mom knows was invited to the wedding. I think it was just kind of humiliating to her. And confusing. And heartbreaking. I'm hoping she won't be too upset for too long and that she'll realize that George was always a little bit of a dud and that she deserves so much more. But right now is a sensitive time."

". . ."

"Gwen?"

"Hm? Yes? What's that?"

"You look . . ."

"Sorry?"

"You look a little something. Are you car sick?"

"Car sick? No! Um. No, I'm fine."

"Then, what's that look for?"

"Oh. Uh. Nothing. Um. I was just absorbing your mom's story. It's really sad. I feel bad. George sounds like a *total dick*."

"I mean . . . the story is that he just fell in love at first sight. So . . . I don't know. Maybe he's not a dick and just a victim to cupid's arrow?"

"You sound skeptical."

"Well, the part I didn't mention is that there's a forty-year age difference. And George is very rich."

"Oh."

"Yeah. I don't want to sound like I think age differences are always about money, because obviously they're not. And maybe I'm just a frowny skeptic and he and this woman are in the purest love you could find. But . . . my mom got dumped for someone thirty-five years younger than her and . . . it just hurts. She's hurting. Ah . . . sorry. I didn't mean to get worked up."

"This is probably not consolation at all, but it honestly sounds like she's better off without George."

"No, she definitely is. Like I said before, he was never Mr. Romance. And she's already been so much more active and excited about activities than she ever was when they were together. But still . . . break-ups are tough."

"I'm *so* sorry, Sam."

"Oh . . . Wow."

"Hm?"

"You *actually* sound sorry. And not just in a commiseration sort of way."

"I am. I am so sorry."

"Are you sure you're okay? You seriously look a little green around the gills."

"Okay. I have to tell you something—*Whoa! Look out!!!!*"

"Oh, shit!"

"What the hell *was* that? Pull over! Pull over!"

"Okay, pulling over. Wow. Can you see it from here? Everything's all right. I think it was just a box people were trying not to hit. Wait! What are you doing?"

"I just . . . I think I should pull it out of the road."

"What?! Gwen! It's just a box! Let it get hit instead of you."

"No . . . I don't think that was just a box."

"Gwen! Wait!"

"I'll wait for a break in traffic. I won't get hit. I swear."

"Hold on. Gwen, this is way too dangerous."

"Sam, I might have seen wrong but I swear there were—Here's a break in traffic! I'm grabbing it! . . . Thanks! You didn't have to come too."

"I'm not going to let you run onto the parkway by yourself just to grab a—Holy shit."

"I knew it! Get it over to the side."

"Here. I'll carry it. Let's get back by the car. The hazards are blinking. It'll be safer over there."

"Good idea, Sam."

"I . . . cannot believe I'm carrying a box of *kittens* right now."

"They're so *little*. How many are there?"

"Four? No, five. How the heck did you see that this was a box of kittens? We were going, like, sixty miles an hour."

"I have no idea. I just saw one little head poke up and I knew what it was. I didn't know how many there were though."

"How did they get into the middle of the parkway?"

"They fell out of someone's truck or something? Or . . . or someone left them? Ugh. I don't even want to think about that."

"Yeah. Gosh. How could someone leave them? Oh! Look at the little beans on that one's paw. They're so pink."

"You're as susceptible to cat-paw beans as the next guy, huh? Oh, Sam, what are we going to do with them?"

"Well, you might have to squish your feet to one side, but unfortunately, I think that's our best option. The backseat is way too full of Danny's kitchen stuff."

"You . . . you're saying that we're going to take them with us?"

". . . Are you kidding me? Of course! You think I would watch you run into speeding traffic to rescue kittens only to leave them on the side of the road? No way. Besides, we're on a ticking clock here. We need to get back to the city. Let's bring the kittens with us and we can call a shelter on the way and figure out what the best course of action is."

"I . . . okay."

"All right. Hold on to the kittens while I merge. I'm really gonna have to gun it."

". . ."

". . ."

"I thought you said you were gonna have to gun it."

"I *am* gunning it. These are apparently the biggest guns that Danny's car has."

"Okay, oh, my gosh, I'm just gonna sit here and hope we don't get mowed down. Kittens, don't watch!"

"Aaaaaaand we're safely merged. Piece of cake. I have some water in my bag."

"Huh? Oh, I'm fine. I have a water bottle too."

"Not for you. For the cats."

"Oh! Ha. Um . . . I don't know if cats this young drink water?"

"Do you think they're all from the same litter? They all look so different."

"I know. Look at the little orange one. I love cats with a pink nose. They just kill me."

"Does Garpy have a pink nose?"

"No. He's a black cat, green eyes."

"Ah. Very mystical and mysterious."

"He'd like to think so. Oh no. Sam."

"What's wrong?"

"I'm falling in love."

"Oh, yeah?"

"This is a nightmare. I can't be a lady with six cats. I have a life. A job. I travel."

"Quick! Call a shelter and figure out how we can start a college fund for them. That way we won't feel so bad about dropping them off somewhere."

"Right, right. Okay. Lemme . . . do . . . some research."

"Find anything?"

"Yeah. Lots actually. I'm gonna make some calls."

Chapter Twelve

"Wowzers. I never want to make another polite phone call again."

"Yeah, Gwen. That was a LOT of phone calls. You have a very professional phone voice, by the way."

"I know. I can't help it. It's a reflex. And a curse. I think my vocal cords are going to freeze up."

"Well, any luck? It sounded like maybe that last place?"

"I've got good news and bad news."

"Can't it ever just be good news with us?"

"I think we're experiencing the full spectrum that life has to offer today. You want the bad or the good first?"

"The good."

"Well, the good news is that there is a shelter that will take them, last minute, on a Sunday afternoon, miracle of miracles. They'll provide an exam and any inoculations and shots and stuff that they might need."

"That's great! . . . What's the bad news?"

"The bad news is twofold. One: they literally don't have space to house them overnight. And two: if we want to get them in for an exam today, we have to get them there in the next forty-five minutes."

"Oh, boy. Dare I even ask where this shelter is?"

"Well, that's actually a skosh of good news. They're in Harlem."

"So, they're on the way? That's perfect! Here, put the address into maps."

"It looks like we could jussst make it there. By the skin of our teeth. But it's gonna add fifteen minutes to our ETA."

"Which cuts your window of padding down to only half an hour. Putting you at Florine's before Shaw—"

"By *maybe* fifteen minutes. Yeah. It's shit. The whole thing is total shit."

"Well, we don't *have* to bring the kittens there, do we?"

"You heard how many calls I just made. Ten? Fifteen? That was every shelter in the city limits. They don't take random drop-offs on a Sunday night."

"Do . . . do you think they have to get dropped off tonight? I could take them home for the night and figure it out tomorrow."

"No way. First of all, you have your date tonight. You can't bring a box of kittens to your Katie McConnick date. Second of all, and I probably should have made this a first of all, these are *really* young kittens. We don't know what to feed them or if they're sick or traumatized. You really want to be solely responsible for their well-being for an entire night? What if something happened to them?"

"Yeah. Good point. But I don't think I have time to drop you off and then circle back up and make it in time."

"I know."

"So, you're saying that you're willing to take a hit for the kittens and maybe not make it in time to the interview?"

"I mean . . . didn't you see the paw-beans? They're *pink*, Sam."

"I'll take that as a yes."

"Luckily, it doesn't look like there's any traffic. I think, no, I'm *deciding* that this is all gonna work out."

"Just like that?"

"I've got my good luck marble, my good luck man, some

good luck kittens. You've done, like, fifty good deeds today. I just ran into high-speed traffic to rescue these cats . . . Yeah, I think we'll be rewarded handsomely for all this karma we've been churning up."

"Your good luck man?"

". . ."

"Is that me?"

". . ."

"Am I the good luck man?"

"Just *shhhh* over there."

"Oh, I'm sorry, is it a secret?"

"Shhh!"

"Oh, now there's a library-shushing finger involved. I guess you mean business."

". . ."

"You really don't want to answer any questions about this good luck man thing, huh?"

". . ."

"All right, I'll let you be mysterious and quiet. Meanwhile, I'll just be over here inferring my *ass* off."

". . ."

"Seriously, I'm going to infer my way so far down the rabbit hole I won't even be able to see the little dot of light at the top anymore."

"Knock yourself out."

"I'm going to read between the lines so aggressively I'll get astigmatism."

"You definitely don't understand what astigmatism is."

"Who needs general knowledge when I've got all this good luck?"

"These are the kinds of things people say right before they walk face first into a glass door."

"Are you wishing bad luck on your good luck man? Right

before we enter the city limits and fight our way through traffic? That's a pretty risky move."

"I think you can handle it. Just don't drive over any glass. How's our gas level? We're not going to run out, are we?"

"We're good. Still have plenty. Seriously, though, aren't you relieved we finally made it to the Bronx? We're back in the city!"

"I've lived in this city long enough to know that if you're a borough away from your destination, you might as well be a state away from your destination."

"Yeah . . . I was trying to look on the bright side, but that is unfortunately true. Oh, look! The leopard-print one is yawning."

"Leopard print? That's called calico."

"Oh. Right. I don't know much about cats."

"Calico would be a nice name for a cat. You could call him Cal."

"I could, but Vera's boyfriend is named Cal so that would be a little bit weird."

"You took that very literally . . . Are you . . . considering adopting one of these cats?"

"Don't say things like that in front of them! I don't want them to get their hopes up!"

"Sam, I don't think they speak English."

"Right, right. They're just babies."

"And they're *cats*."

"Hey, has anyone ever proved definitively that cats *can't* speak English?"

"Well, if there was any animal that was fluent in English but pretended not to be for strategic reasons, it would definitely be cats."

"The answer to your question is m-a-y-b-e. I can't remember if I'm in a no-pets building or not. So, I have to check my lease. Are *you* considering it?"

"I . . . I can't. Carl the catsitter has been very clear that Garpy is his limit. There's no way I could get another cat and keep my current situation afloat. I just travel too much for another cat."

"You could always ask . . . someone else to take care of them, couldn't you?"

"I don't like burdening people. No In Case of Emergency, remember? No, it's better to just keep things like they are. I'm not the right owner for this little guy. No matter how much I want to boop his little perfectly pink nose. I'll just take a few photos to commemorate this moment."

"Hey, Gwen? Can I ask something random?"

"Shhhh! I think the kitties are sleeping."

"Oh. Sorry! Wait, do I actually have to whisper? Does human talking bother a sleeping kitten?"

"Oh. No. Now that you mention it, probably not. Go ahead."

"It's just that . . . I've been noticing for a while . . . You're not wearing any jewelry."

"Yes . . ."

"Well, I was thinking about that in the flea market. Because I was trying to find a good luck charm for you and I came across those charm bracelets. At first I thought, *Oh! This would be perfect for her.* But then I thought about it and realized that you don't wear any jewelry at all."

"Right . . ."

"And your nails aren't painted."

"Uh huh."

"And, I guess, for someone who photographs other people's adornments for a living it's a little surprising to me that you don't wear any jewelry. Or have any visible tattoos. Or . . . there aren't even any shiny clips in your hair."

"You know that metal bra and underwear set that Princess Leia wears in *Star Wars*?"

"Yes . . ."

"I'm wearing that under my clothes."

". . ."

"Hahahhahaha!!!! Sam, I'm just kidding. You should see your face right now."

"Without even checking, I'm sure I'm giving you full Dumbfounded Doofus right now."

"For the record, I really was joking."

"It's probably better for my blood pressure that I believe you."

"So, you want to know why I don't wear any jewelry?"

"If it's not too personal and you want to tell me."

"Well, first of all, it's smarter as a traveler not to wear a lot of attention-grabbing jewelry. People can learn a lot about you observing that kind of stuff. And over the years I've learned that being lower profile is usually a good thing when traveling alone as a woman."

"Ah. That makes sense. But what about when you're in NYC? Do you wear stuff then?"

"I used to. A lot. Rings and earrings and necklaces. I used to have an eyebrow piercing. See? You can still see the little mark here over my right eye. But . . . the more I talked to people about why they chose to wear *their* jewelry . . . the less important mine started to seem to me."

"How so?"

"Well, a lot of the time, this stuff really means something to people."

"You mean in a wedding-ring sort of way?"

"Well, sure. People wear jewelry to show fidelity and commitment. But there are a lot of unexpected reasons too. Sobriety chips and in memoriam tattoos. Some people wear their loved one's dog tags. Or their mom's college ring. Or earrings their aunt got them for graduating high school."

"And you don't have anything like that?"

"No. My biological mom didn't leave anything behind, and . . . my parents aren't sentimental like that. They never really gave us those kinds of gifts. I've had a boyfriend give me a necklace once. But . . . as soon as we broke up, it became meaningless to me. There are other reasons people wear jewelry. It's not all sentimental. Style choices and image choices and armor and deflection and for good energy or good health or luck or karma. Religious reasons, superstitious ones. All these different reasons and rationales. But I . . . have just never felt strongly enough about any of it. So. Here I am. No jewelry. No tattoos. Just . . ."

"You."

"Hm?"

"You're just *you*. I like that."

". . ."

"Not that people who wear jewelry and whatnot are *not* themselves. It's just that you are definitely you."

"That is . . . an extremely sweet interpretation."

"You know, I went into my mom's room to grab a box of hats off the top shelf that she couldn't reach and I saw, on her dresser, her wedding ring. She keeps it in a little velvet box."

"Oh, wow. Did it make you sad to see it?"

"Mmm. More nostalgic than anything. I remember that ring on her finger so clearly from my childhood. I used to sit in her lap and she'd let me twist it around. It's simple. Just a gold band. So was his, I think. But he was buried with his."

"How long did she wear it after he died?"

"All the way up until my high school graduation. And then she moved it to a necklace. And then, one day, I didn't see it anymore. I knew she wouldn't have thrown it away or something. But I never knew where she kept it. And then I saw it in its box this weekend, open, like she'd been looking at it. And I just thought to myself . . . she's all torn up over George and you know who she turned to for comfort? My dad. Even after all these years. Even when her pain is over a different romantic relationship, my dad is still the one who can get her through the hard times."

"That is so . . ."

"Sad?"

"I was going to say lovely. Your mom seems like someone who loves very hard."

"She is. As evidenced by the extreme sport she's turned mothering into."

". . . Are . . . are you the same way?"

"Do I love hard? I . . . think so. I've never had the kind of romance that my parents had. But . . ."

"You'll do anything for your friends. And clearly you'll do *anything* for your mom."

"Do you? Love hard?"

"I'd like to. Who wouldn't? But, I . . . haven't had much practice."

"Ummmm, am I going straight here?"

"Yes. No! Veer left. Yup. Now merge with that lane. Ah! Don't hit that car."

"Solid advice."

"And then get back in the right lane because we're going to have to—yup, you got it. Oh, wow. We're almost there. To the shelter."

"Yeah, we made really good time. Which is unreal, considering this is Sunday afternoon traffic we're talking here. I must really be your good luck man."

". . ."

"Are you ignoring me again?"

"Clearly."

"Okay . . . fair enough . . . Parking, parking, parking, gonna have to find parking so that we can drop these kitties off. Ah! Perfect."

"Are you sure you can fit in this spot? It's pretty small—wow. Aaaaand ya just did it."

"Yeah. Parallel parking is ninety percent believing you can do it."

"Not gonna lie, that was hot."

"Oh."

"You even did the one-hand-on-the-back-of-my-headrest thing. That's lethal."

"Oh. Ah. I wasn't—"

"Trying to be hot? Yeah, that's what they all say."

"No, really—"

"We don't have time to quibble about unintentional hotness! Let's get these kitties to safety!"

"Um. Yes. Okay. Priorities. Right."

Chapter Thirteen

"Gwen, they're gonna be all right."

"But they just took them away."

"They were supposed to take them away. They were the veterinarians."

"They were so small. Didn't they seem smaller once we went into the clinic?"

"They're very young. But now they're in very safe hands."

"I know, I just—"

"Gwen. Game face. Niles Shaw. Florine Weatherbell. Your book deal."

"Right! Right. I know you're right."

"The kittens will be waiting for us after you totally kick Niles Shaw's ass."

"You really have some pent-up ire for Niles Shaw."

"If I ever meet him I hope he's walking on a sidewalk below me while I happen to have a bucket of cold water in my hands."

"I . . . would pay to see that."

"Okay. Let's get down there. With any luck, you'll have a little over a half an hour."

"Oh, shit."

"What's wrong? Should I pull over?"

"No! No, it's just that Shaw posted an update about half an hour ago. His flight landed at JFK."

"Okay. Okay. Don't panic. We knew that his flight had to land at some point. And better JFK than LGA. At least he's further away. Say he got in a cab at that exact second, he'd still at least be as far as we are. We're totally gonna be . . ."

"You have *got* to be kidding me."

"Okay, maybe it's not as bad as it looks."

"It *looks* like wall-to-wall traffic."

"Let me just check maps and see if there's an alternate route . . ."

". . ."

". . ."

"I take it from your silence that there isn't."

"Apparently there was an accident on the FDR so all the traffic has rerouted and . . ."

"The train? Should I jump on the train? I could get . . . the B? The C?"

"I . . . think that's gonna take at least forty-five minutes. Especially if it's running on whatever random weekend schedule it's running on."

"Oh, my God. *All of that*. We went through *all of that* and now NYC traffic is gonna be what wrecks this?"

"Wait! Look! Gwen!"

"What?"

"City Bikes."

"What? No. Sam."

"Trust me! This is perfect! I just have to find a place to park and . . . right here!"

"Sam, this is an illegal parking zone!"

"There's so much traffic, no one is going around handing out tickets right now."

"Yeah, you're right, they'll probably just jump straight to towing you."

"Well, we all have to take risks in life."

"With your friend's car?"

"He'd understand. Are you getting out or not? Don't forget your bag!"

"Sam."

"Okay, hold on. I have the app for these bikes. Let me just rent them and—"

"Sam. SAM!"

"Huh?"

"First of all, we're *so* far away from Florine's."

"Hence the bikes."

"Second of all, I can't show up drenched in sweat. Seriously, it would be better to just not show up at all than looking like I swam there. And THIRDLY AND MOST IMPORTANTLY, I can't ride a bike."

"You can't ride a bike."

"Never learned."

"Okay. Well . . . the first problem is intractable. Yes, we're very far. But the second two problems can be solved at once."

"How?"

"I'll put you on the handlebars."

"You'll put me on the . . . *what?*"

"I'll ride the bike and balance you on the handlebars. We'll get there in no time. Look, you can see from the topography map that a lot of it is downhill, okay?"

"You want me to . . ."

"It'll be really easy. I swear. And you won't get sweaty. Let me just get it out of the dock thingy . . . There. And then, here, put your backpack on your front and . . ."

"AND WHAT?"

"Okay, you seem understandably tense, but trust me, this is all going to work out. Gwen . . . I am going to be *so* careful. I would never, ever, let you get hurt."

"I—How am I supposed to get up there?"

"Here. It's easy. One arm around my neck and I'll just pick you up and there we go."

"EEP!"

"The trick is that you have to use me like a chair. Put your back against my chest and actually lean your weight so that I can balance us. You can rest your head back on my shoulder. Perfect. Just like that. You're doing great."

"Oh. Hi."

"Hi."

"I'm very scared of this plan."

"I'll be so, so careful. You won't have to worry about a thing. See?"

"EEEEEEP!"

"Here we go. Just gently cruising. No big deal. Nothing to see here."

"What happens if we see a cop?"

"Um . . . We tell them you're in labor and that I'm rushing you to the hospital."

"In labor with what? My backpack?"

"Yes. We're very excited. We're going to name it Brenda Junior."

"Banana man!"

"Huh?"

"Watch out for the banana man!"

"Oh. Wow. Ha. You mean the man selling bananas."

"What else would I have meant?"

"Well, when someone shouts the words *banana man* at you, your brain offers an array of possibilities."

"Sam."

"Yeah?"

"This is not downhill."

"This part isn't, but look, once we get there, it is."

"How're your glutes doing back there?"

"I'm not sure anyone has ever checked on the well-being of my ass before."

"Well, no one has ever biked me a million blocks uphill before, so I thought I should check in."

"Don't worry. See? Ah . . . now we can cruise a little."

"Open up."

"Huh?"

"I have a water bottle. I'm going to give you some."

"Oh. I have to stop at this stoplight anyhow."

"Should I get off?"

"Why?"

"Isn't it hard to balance me on the bike when we're not moving?"

"No, but it would be easier if I . . . Can I put my arm here?"

"Sure. Now, it's really like you're a proud papa cupping the backpack baby. Brenda Junior."

"Light of my life."

"Okay, wow, this part is like, a proper downhill. Oh, boy. I can't look. Oh, my God."

"I told you, Gwen. I won't go too fast. I seriously will not put you in danger. See? Here we go, nice and easy . . . Are you covering your eyes?"

"Distract me! Ask me questions or something!"

"Okay, what's the number one thing you want to talk to Florine Weatherbell about?"

"She left a man at the altar in 1974 and then, as far as the public knows, never dated again. She left the country and went to Madrid for four years. When she came back, she allegedly had over twenty thousand developed original photos in her luggage."

"Wow."

"I'm obviously not going to pry unless she willingly brings it up, but yeah, I'm curious about those circumstances. And those photos. I want to see some of them."

"They haven't been displayed like her pictures of famous people at parties?"

"Nope. Never. Some people call them her lost years. I'm so curious. Were they portraits? Nature photography? Animals? Food? Architecture? Everything? All of the above? Was she documenting her stay or trying to shoot something completely different?"

"Twenty thousand over the course of four years."

"It means she was taking dozens a day, probably. And then either developing that many a day or developing by the hundreds every week or so. She must've had a dark room in her apartment. Just the sheer amount of time she would have had to spend there . . ."

"Oh, man. Now I'm curious. I wish I could come to this interview."

"Well, you can read all about it in my book."

"I cannot *wait* to read your book. I want a signed copy."

"No way."

"Why?! I'm biking you to your appointment, remember? Don't you think that should earn me a signed copy?"

"No, I just mean that my signature is ridiculous. I won't be signing anyone's copy."

"Well, practice then, because I want a signed copy."

"Oh, finally another stoplight."

"You're still scared?"

"No. Not really. I just want you to have a break."

"I'm all right. We're making good time."

"Hey, Mama, you two heading to get married or something?"

"Huh?"

"The only time I see a man balance a woman on the handlebars is when he's rushing her to the courthouse."

"Ha. No. We're not . . ."

"Well, you better get on it, son. A pretty lady like that and somebody is gonna be biking her to the courthouse. And you too, Mama. If you've got a man who will bike you around on his handlebars, you better lock it down. You want some mango?"

"Oh. Yeah. Hold on. Lemme get my cash . . . Oh, thanks Sam."

"Here you go. Good luck, you two."

"Bye! Thanks for paying, Sam. Ripe mango on a stick is one of my favorite things about New York."

"Do me a favor and don't put that pointy stick in your mouth until we're at another stoplight."

"Oh. Yes. Good point. It's funny that he thought you were racing me off to get married."

"Funny? I dunno. I kinda get it. We're all snuggled up and clearly hopped up on adrenaline."

"Oh. Yeah."

"Mango break."

"Oh. Right. Yum. Oh, it's perfectly ripe. Here. Want a bite?"

"Mmm. Wow."

"We're getting close, huh?"

"Almost there. Are you done with the stick? I'll throw it in the trash."

"Wow. Got it in one."

"I'm feeling lucky today."

"No comment."

"Because I'm the Good Luck Man."

"Lord help me."

"Sorry. Couldn't help myself."

"Try to tone down that particular part of your personality on your big date tonight, okay?"

"…"

"…"

"So . . . you really want me to make it tonight, huh?"

"I mean . . ."

"You don't think there's any reason for me to cancel if I could?"

"I mean, Danny's car is probably gonna get towed, so . . . you should probably handle that."

"And I have to pick up our kittens before the vet closes."

"Right. Our kittens."

"So, there's the car and there's the kittens. No other reasons?"

"Why did you stop biking?"

"We're here."

"Oh. We're here. *We're here?* Oh, my God."

"Careful. Here, I'll lift you down."

"I can't believe we're here already."

"Buns of steel over here."

"Apparently. *Man*, I'm glad you sat next to me on the bus."

"Gwen?"

"Yeah?"

"I'm *really* glad I sat next to you on the bus. Listen—"

"Wait. Sam."

"Yeah?"

"Look. Today was . . . today was a really special day. Really special. But . . . there's some stuff that you don't know about me. One thing in particular. And, um . . . I'm just . . . probably headed out of the country again soon. For who knows how long. And look, I think it's just probably best if I say thank you for the ride. *All* the rides. From the bottom of my heart. Thank you. And . . . we'll keep in touch, okay? I'll text you. I'll let you know how the interview goes, okay? I won't leave you hanging. And yeah. Thank you. Thank you so much. Bye, okay? We'll talk soon? And good luck tonight! With Katie. Good luck!"

Chapter Fourteen

Gwen

I take one last look at Sam, sitting there, dumbstruck, on the clunky blue bike, his long legs triangled impossibly far out on the sidewalk, and then, I'm around the corner of the brick building, out of sight, and we are officially no longer on this journey together.

It feels so weird to have said goodbye to Sam.

And like *that*?

Ugh.

Why did I do it like that? I thought tearing off the Band-Aid would be best. A quick goodbye and swift shove in Katie's direction would save me from having to explain too much. But he just looked *confused* and I don't blame him. I mean . . . we have kittens together for God sakes and I booted him down the sidewalk with just a quick thank you!?

It hurts to think of the kittens. And I can't help myself, so I peek back around the side of the building just in time to see his blue hair sail away, back up the block, and he's gone.

He's gone.

Because I sent him away.

He was seconds away from telling me that he'd rather not go on this date with Katie and I sent him away.

Tears prickle hotly at my eyes and I'm wretched. I can still feel him pressed up against me, breathing adorably hard in my ear. His smile pressed against my hair as he pedaled up the hills. And now he's gone.

Off to the life he lived before he met me this morning. And me the same.

Back to my life. The one I love. The one I raced down the eastern seaboard to maintain. The one that defines me. The one that . . .

I take out a compact mirror and quickly fix my makeup. My hair needs another brush. I get my camera out, proudly wearing it on my hip, wanting it to be the first thing Florine notices about me.

And I'm ready. Here I am. Curiosity in hand, all my other emotions pushed down the chute. I've gotta focus. Chance of a lifetime, remember?

Why is it that the chance of a lifetime feels just a little less special on a day that I happened to sit next to Sam on a bus?

On a deep exhale that's meant to shove away any and all uncertainty, I round the corner of the building and head toward Florine's building on sure feet. A dog-walker with ten tiny dogs on leashes scurries past me. Kids walk in hand-holding chains. Glittery people totter past on high heels. People in oversized suits yap into black-beetle cell phones pressed to their ears.

The last gauntlet. Making it down the block to get to Florine's address.

The door to her building is at the far end of the block and it's got the gilded gold archway of old New York. A doorman in a deep red uniform stands at the ready in a patch of setting sunlight on marble stairs. A green awning yawns out over the sidewalk all the way to the street to protect any cab-riders from whatever the weather may be. Even from all the way back here I can tell it's a grand entrance to an even grander building.

I have a ticket inside, I remind myself. She's waiting for me. Florine Weatherbell is waiting for me.

And then, with a stomach-punching dose of reality, I recognize the back of the head fifty feet in front of me. It's a fashionably severe blond cut on a square head. He's got the shoulders of someone who has never once thought he didn't deserve his success. And there's so much jaunt in his steps I wanna scream.

Niles Shaw is about to walk into Florine's building ten seconds before me.

I stop in my tracks for half a second.

No. NO. This can't be happening. I didn't take a bus, walk along the highway, ride in a junker from 1982, then white-knuckle a bike ride all the way down here to get cut in line ten seconds before the finish! Why the hell did I pause to brush my hair????

That's it. I'm not going down without a fight. If I have to fly-tackle him, so be it. I've heard women heal faster than men anyhow. Hopefully Florine will agree to see me with a black eye.

I crouch down into sprint position and I'm off. Every soul-killing muscle-tearing three-mile run at top speed comes home to roost. I was made to sprint short distances and Niles Shaw doesn't know he's about to lose this race.

But then, something whizzes past my right elbow. Something speedy and blue.

My eyes widen and I stop running as Sam, on his bike, perfect, lovely Sam, weaves through pedestrians, skirts an ice-cream cart, and comes to a screeching halt in front of Niles Shaw. I'm too far back to hear what he says, but Sam does a comically big double-take and lunges for Shaw's hand. He's pumping it up and down and giving him puppy-dog eyes.

Shaw tries to pull away but Sam is holding him in place. For one, burning second, he makes eye contact with me over Shaw's shoulders and widens his eyes.

He's Gandalf hanging on by his fingertips, about to be dragged to hell. *Run!* he's telling me.

Sam digs a receipt and a pen out of his pocket and hands it to Shaw.

"Oh, my GOD," I mutter to myself as, behind Shaw's back, I show the doorman the email invitation from Florine's granddaughter. Sam, who wants nothing more than to dump ice water on Shaw's head from two stories up, is shaking his hand and begging for an autograph.

To give me a head start.

For the second time in four minutes I feel the awful, unnatural velcro rip of running away from Sam.

But there's no way I'm spoiling this chance. I'm on the elevator. I'm pressing 15. The doors are closing. And there's Shaw. I see his whole scowling face. And then three inches of it and then one inch. And then he's gone. And I'm racing upward.

Chapter Fifteen

Sam

I know, I know, ultra-marathons. I can do hard physical stuff. I'm an athlete. Yadda yadda.

Well, nothing, and I mean *nothing* has prepared me for sprint-biking a seventy-pound tourist cruiser fifty blocks in one direction with precious cargo balancing neatly on my handlebars, waylaying a sworn enemy, and then biking fifty blocks back. By the time I'm swerving around the banana man for the second time I'm sure I've lost about ten pounds in water weight and my legs and I are no longer on speaking terms.

I'm three blocks, two blocks, and one. There it is. Danny's junker absorbing the setting sun like a grubby penny stuck in the crack of a sidewalk. I made it.

Yup, I made it just in time to notice the tow truck beep-beep-beeping in reverse to hitch the car up.

"Wait!" I shout, making one last effort on this cursed bike. I skid up to the tow truck driver's door. "Wait! I'm here! I'm here!"

"Good for you," the driver says, squinting through the smoke of his cigarette to line the tow truck up correctly.

"Please don't tow this car. I'm here. I'll take it away right now. It'll be like I was never here. I swear."

"Yeah. And then I don't get paid. Beat it."

I'm frantic. "I'll pay you! Cold hard cash. Or . . . do you have a Venmo?"

The driver gives me a look like the word Venmo makes him want to crush my city bike under the wheel of his truck.

"No?" I try a different tactic. "Okay, how about this. If I don't get in this car and race downtown, I'm going to miss an opportunity with the most incredible girl in the world. Seriously. You don't know how long I've been waiting for a girl like this."

"You're barking up the wrong tree, kid. My divorce was finalized last month."

I sag . . . and then rally. There's one last tactic. And if it doesn't work, then nothing will. I dig out my phone and pull up my photos. "Look!"

"What the hell is that?"

"It's a box of kittens. Aren't they cute?"

He blinks. Then he flicks his cigarette butt away and reaches down from the driver's seat to take my phone. He blinks again. "Yeah. Actually, they are."

"Well, if I don't get to the vet in the next fifteen minutes then I don't know what'll happen to these kittens."

(I do know. They send them to a willing foster family for the night and I get fined for leaving them there. Then I can pick them up in the morning. But there's no way I'm lowering the stakes for the sake of honesty at a moment like this.)

"These are your kittens?"

"We found them in a box on the side of the highway and brought them to the vet to make sure they were healthy. Now I'm trying to find homes for them."

He clears his throat. Scratches the back of his neck. Gives a great, long-suffering sigh. "Is the black one with the white paws spoken for?"

I cannot believe my ears. Or my luck, or . . . anything. "No!

He's yours! You want him? Give me your number! I'll make sure to get him to you as soon as possible!"

He digs around in his glove compartment and comes up with a business card. As he's handing it over, he doesn't let go of one corner. "If you go back on this deal, I can make your life with that car very difficult, you understand?"

A shiver runs down my spine. "The cat is yours."

He gives me an appraising look, hands me the card, puts the truck in drive, and pulls away.

I sag against the bike in relief. But not for long, because I actually don't have any time. I run the city bike to the kiosk (on legs made of string cheese) and ka-chink it into its little spot. And then I'm revving Danny's car and squealing it ten blocks to the vet. I arrive just as the receptionist is locking the front door.

"Oh, thank GOD," she mutters when she sees me. She's back moments later with a ream of paperwork, a bill that makes my eyes water, and a plastic carrying case that's filled with sleeping kittens.

Fifteen minutes later I'm standing on the sidewalk with my arms full of kittens, my legs screaming for dear life, my heart heavy and confused. All at once, everything swamps over me. The adrenaline of the day is wearing away, and . . . I realize that not only did I meet someone and form real feelings for her today, I also got turned down. And set up with someone else. And then I amazing-raced from Boston to New York and did a five-mile bike sprint. And became a cat father.

And now? I look at the time and realize that I am officially minutes away from standing Katie up.

That's it. That's the last straw. Is this the life I'd like to be leading? Dumped by one woman, pressured by another, standing up yet another while holding a box of cats on the road?

When I woke up this morning, this is not the Sam Champion I pictured being by the end of the day.

First things first.

This time I mean it. I'm not screwing around anymore. If I don't get my mom on the phone in the next twenty seconds, I'm seriously going to lose my shit. She's been pulling strings all day and all it's done is tie me up.

I broke my leg, I text my mom. *I'm in the hospital.*

Less than one inhale later and she's finally calling me back.

"Sammy? Sam?"

"Ma, I'm fine. I'm not in the hospital. It was just to get you to call me."

"What the hell? Why would you *ever* text me something like that, you almost gave me a—"

"It's completely unacceptable for you to avoid my phone calls. I would never do that to you, you'd completely freak out if I did, so you are not allowed to do that to me. For any reason. Especially because you're just trying to get your way. It's not fair. And it really pisses me off."

"*Sam!*"

"Well, it does."

"I . . . You're right. It's not fair. I'm sorry. I was just trying—"

"To prevent me from canceling on Katie. I know."

"Do you have any idea how hard I worked to get you this date? It took some real gymnastics on my end. And she's a wonderful girl. And you've liked her for so long. I just thought it would be such a shame if you canceled it."

"No, Ma, I haven't."

"You haven't what?"

"Liked her for so long."

"Don't be ridiculous. In high school you used to—"

"In high school. Yes. *I had a crush in high school.* But I honestly haven't thought of Katie in years. There's no torch. I'm sure she's great. And, you know, if I ran into her or something I would like to catch up with her and see how she's doing. But

I don't need a date. Why is everyone so convinced I need a date with her?!"

"Who is everyone?"

"Huh?"

"You said everyone."

"I—my friend. The one I told you about. She's convinced I need to tell Katie how I felt in high school to . . . I don't know . . . complete the circle or something. Everyone wants me on this date so badly I'm seriously about to lose my shit."

". . . Because you don't want to go on this date."

"Right."

"And not for the usual reasons."

"The usual reasons?"

"Yeah, that you get embarrassed to have your mother set you up on a date and that you'd rather meet someone, in your words, *organically*, and that you think it's awkward to date someone who your mother has already decided you should marry."

"Oh. Wow. You . . . actually have an accurate read on the usual reasons."

"I'm a smart woman, Sam. I just . . . ignored that part because I thought it was better to give you a little push."

"No pushes necessary, all right? I'm thirty years old. I . . . can push myself, okay?"

". . . All right. So, if it's not the usual reasons for not wanting to go on the date with Katie, then what is it?"

". . ."

"Sammy? Are you there?"

"Ma, what do you think about Iceland?"

"What?"

"There's apparently glaciers and hiking and camping and whale-watching and stuff like that."

"Sounds expensive."

"But if we could afford it. Would you want to go?"

"Wait. Are you *inviting* me to Iceland?"

"Yeah. Gwen says she thinks you'd love it."

"Gwen Cellar. Your seatmate."

"Yeah."

"The friend who wants you to date Katie."

"Yeah."

"She thinks I'd love Iceland."

"Focus, Ma. What do you think about a big trip like that?"

"I've never even left the States."

"Me either. But I was thinking that maybe I should . . . Look, I want to go to New Orleans. Over the long weekend coming up. Were you expecting me to come up and stay with you? Because if you were, I can see if Aunt Laura would come down for a couple days so you wouldn't—"

"I don't need you to plan my social calendar, Sam."

"I'm just saying that I don't want to leave you high and dry."

"Of course you wouldn't leave me high and dry! You're the most devoted son I've ever met. My friends at the hiking club can't believe it when they hear how often you visit. You want to go to New Orleans? You don't have to clear it with me. And I can call Aunt Laura on my own. You don't need to call Aunt Laura on my behalf *ever*, you know."

"Oh . . . does it . . . bother you when I call Aunt Laura on your behalf?"

". . . I know you mean well, but it makes me feel about ninety-five years old. I'm not so fragile that I can't call my sister to make plans when I'm lonely. I have a life, you know. You're a huge part of it, but, sweetie, you are certainly not *all* of it."

"Oh . . . Huh."

"What's wrong?"

"Nothing . . . I just . . . kind of thought I *was* all of it. So . . . I'm relieved. And . . . disoriented? I feel weird."

"You didn't tell me why you're canceling on Katie."

"You can't guess?"

"Of course I can guess. You've been clear as glass your entire life, sweetie. I just wanted to make sure *you* know."

"Yeah. I know."

"Then why do you sound so sad about it?"

"I'm not sure she feels the same way. We just parted ways and she kind of . . . gave me the boot."

"Of course she feels the same way."

"Ma—"

"Sammy, don't give me that. You're tall, you have a nice face, and you'd do anything for anybody. Does she have a man?"

"No. She's single."

"Great. Then she feels the same way."

"That doesn't mean she wants to *date*. She said that she was going away soon and that there was something I didn't know about her. So . . . yeah, I don't even know what to do about that."

"I just texted you Katie's contact information. Be sweet when you cancel on her."

"Oh! Thanks, Ma! Of course I'll be sweet. I . . . thank you."

"Of course you'll be sweet. Now, I want to talk about this Iceland idea a little more. But first, there's something I have to tell you about this Gwen person."

"Huh?"

"There's nothing you can't find out on the internet, sweetie."

Chapter Sixteen

Gwen

To be blunt, this is the oddest apartment I've ever been in.

Florine's granddaughter, Simona—late teens, tiny, stylish glasses, amber-brown skin and a long braid of curly black hair—lets me in after my tentative knock-nuh-knock.

"Oh, good, I'm glad it was you who made it first," she tells me with a bright smile. "G-ma likes the other guy more, but he seems like a total douche to me."

I'm buoyed by someone, anyone, referring to Niles Shaw as a douche. And completely deflated by the fact that apparently Florine likes him better.

"Come in, come in. G-ma's in the parlor, but she said she wanted me to give you the looky-loo tour first so that you wouldn't be angling for a peek the entire interview. So. Yeah. Here we go."

Simona takes me around the apartment and I gape in awe. It is . . . an apartment made of closets. And I'm not exaggerating. Florine has turned almost every single room into a closet. So, yes, technically, the closets have closets. There's a closet for clothes, of course. And I spot an entire Dior wall, kitty-corner to an entire Chanel wall, which butts up against what I think might be an Oscar de la Renta wall. But there are also closets for the framed artworks that are stacked up because apparently she just has too much to display.

"Those are the Warhols," Simona says, gesturing to a stack about three feet high. "And I think that's a Jackson Pollock." This one is leaned against the wall, the frame backwards, so I'd only be able to confirm if I touched it. Which I won't.

There's a room for historical artifacts, with everything from golden forks to wooden masks carefully enclosed in tiny glass cases.

There's an instruments room and a jam-packed library and a room with the skeletons of at least thirty darkened Tiffany stained-glass lamps. The kitchen is shockingly small and incredibly tidy. The same goes for the two bathrooms that Simona shows me.

"It's so clean in here," I note, marveling at the manpower it would take to dust every cranny of this mausoleum.

"Yeah. There's like fifty cleaners that come once a week. It's total BS, what people say about nobody in or out of her house. Our family comes over. Some of her friends. She goes out too, every once in a while. But it's a better story if she's been a recluse for thirty years, I guess. Here's her room."

Simona opens a set of green gilded doors and I enter the Queen's bedroom. A bed so tall there's a literal step stool next to it. It's a four-poster bed with velvet curtains drawn back to reveal what must surely be a silk bedspread. There are floor-to-ceiling windows leading out to a small balcony that, based on our location, likely has a killer view of the Met and the park.

Besides the bed and the monstrously large mirror on one wall, the bedroom, like the kitchen, is surprisingly sparse and quite tidy. Florine clearly keeps her things confined to closets and out of her actual living space.

Simona leads us through the bedroom and through another

set of double doors. We burst into a shockingly bright room, everything white on white and glowing orange in the setting sun.

And there she is. My enigmatic hero, Florine Weatherbell, sitting straight at a pure white card table, playing with an almost blinding set of white cards. She's wearing, you guessed it, white pants, a white silk shirt, and has a white cardigan tied around her shoulders. Her swing of salt and pepper hair is a shock. She turns to greet me, her face weathered and lovely and touched with just the right amount of makeup. And she immediately frowns. "You didn't take any photographs, did you? Simona, she wasn't supposed to take any photographs."

"I didn't, ma'am. I would never do that without your permission."

"I was hoping it would be the other one instead of you. Shaw."

"Yes. That's what Simona mentioned."

"He's very handsome."

"Well, if it's any consolation, that's his only positive attribute. He's totally boring to talk to. He never asks the right questions."

"Heh. And you do?"

"Well, I'm sure there are lots of 'right' questions. And I'm sure I only ask some of them. But I don't think I'm boring."

"Hm."

"What are you playing?"

"Obviously solitaire."

"Ah. Um. Can I sit?"

"Yes. Right there. Simona, you can go, dear. I'll call if I need anything. Mwah."

"She seems to have her head on straight."

"Simona? Yes. She's far more level-headed than most adults I know."

"Is she the child of your son or daughter?"

"You did your research. My son. They were illegitimate, you know. My children. Never married. Of course that was the height of style back then. Affairs with different people and no one knows who the fathers are."

"Um. Did you? Know?"

"This is an example of a 'right' question?"

"Sorry. No. That's none of my business. That was an example of my insatiable curiosity. Sorry."

"So. You're a writer and a photographer and a world traveler. I've done a bit of all those things."

"Yes, I know. Well, I know some of it at least. I should probably mention that I'm a huge fan of your photography work. You've been a big inspiration to me."

"An inspiration to you? That's interesting. I didn't notice a drop of my influence in your style when Simona showed me your little internet blog thing."

"Oh. Well."

"Well, you might as well show me your camera, then."

"Oh! Of course. Here."

"I hate digital cameras but they fascinate me. What are you even supposed to *do* with all that storage capacity? What a mess. Photos are meant to be developed or lost for ever. Not floating in digital liminal space. But, I suppose if I'd had a digital camera back then I probably would have loved it. What's that there?"

"Um. A green star. My friend embroidered it there."

"Friend? Do friends usually make us blush all the way down our décolletage?"

"Well, I guess he's a friend that I have some feelings for."

"Show me a picture. Like I said, I enjoy looking at a handsome man."

"Oh. Actually, I did take a few pictures of him driving today. Let me find them on the camera . . . here. Here he is."

"The first two are shit. You missed the light. But the third is lovely. He's got a sweet face. That hair is horrendous, though. I'll never understand why someone would want to turn their pallor so sickly."

"I think it's nice on him."

"That's because he makes you blush."

"Maybe. You really don't like it?"

"Oh, I don't like anything. He's handsome. But your camera is horrific. Here. Take it back. I don't even want to hold it anymore. So. You're hoping to leverage this interview into a book deal, hm?"

"Um. Ah. Well—"

"If you are, that's a very smart move."

"Well . . . then. Yes. I guess I am. But that's not the only reason I wanted to meet you. I'm sure you noticed from my blog, but my main interest is in the choices people make in how they adorn themselves and—"

"Yes, yes. You want to see my jewelry collection."

"Well . . . no, actually. I mean, *yes*, I do. Because of that insatiable curiosity issue I mentioned before. But . . . I guess I assumed that you'd actually be *wearing* jewelry. And that's what I'd really be interested in photographing . . . But, I can see that you're not."

"And neither are you."

"You're the second person to notice that today."

"Your blue-haired gent?"

"Yes."

"Well, I've got good news for you. If he's noticing whether or not you're wearing jewelry, he's probably somewhere blushing all the way down his own décolletage over you right now."

"I doubt that."

"Why?"

"He brought me here. To this interview. But I sent him away.

On a date with someone else. Actually, he's probably meeting her right this very second."

"What a waste. Why send him away? You should have brought him up. I'd have fed him ginger cookies."

"It's . . . complicated, I guess?"

"Young people. I hate to break it to you, but literally nothing is complicated for young people. You just think it is."

"Well, it's certainly not simple."

"No, it is simple. Either you're too scared to take a chance, or he is. See? Very simple."

". . ."

"I see you've been struck dumb."

"Well . . . I swear it's more complicated than that."

"Shock me."

"You actually want to hear this?"

"Do I strike you as someone who asks out of politeness?"

"Well, okay . . . I travel the world. All the time. Like, for at least three quarters of the year. He's a total homebody. He spends his vacation days with his mother in Boston. He's never left the States. When would we ever see each other?"

"Yes. It's such a shame that planes don't exist. Also that cell phones have been outlawed. And for the record, you look perfectly miserable when you talk about traveling the world. When did you start to hate it?"

"Hate it? I don't hate it. I love it. It's the most exhilarating, most fulfilling, most . . . It's who I am!"

"Uh huh. Well, sorry to tell you this, but you look sick to death of 'who you are.' And that's why I didn't like your blog. Everything from years ago is wonderful. Filled with light and your own personal wonder. Everything recently seems more like a travel agency's advertisements for timeshares than anything else. Your light's gone out, honey."

". . ."

". . . Simona? Love? Bring out some cookies and something to drink, please. I've just said rude things and I need to make amends."

"You weren't rude. I mean, yes, you were rude. But . . . I'm not sure you're wrong."

"I never insinuated I was wrong."

"My light can't go out for this. It's my job. It's my *life*."

"It would still be your job in New York City, no?"

"I . . . the whole thing is predicated on travel, going to interesting places and meeting interesting people."

"You live in a melting pot."

"Right. Right. I just . . ."

"Think of yourself one way and can't stand to think of yourself in another?"

". . . Yes. Exactly . . . How did you guess that?"

"Honey, I was *the* it girl for almost forty years. And then it all went to shit and I couldn't stand to go to even one more party with all those miserable people. And I stopped and asked myself, *Florine, when are you happiest?* And you know what the answer was? It was when I was alone, in this room. So, I went indoors and I stayed indoors and I didn't come out for almost twelve years. And when I finally did come out, I was an old woman and no one recognized me and I had some peace. Once a week I eat a croissant in the Met café and Simona and I stroll the park. I don't want more than that. It's exactly what I want, so it's what I do."

"Just like that you changed everything?"

"I didn't change everything. It didn't change the past. It didn't take away any of my accomplishments. It simply changed who I allowed myself to be in my own eyes. I'd been scared for years of becoming boring and passé. And then one day I just decided that I live in the most stylish house in New York, surrounded by the most beautiful things, and nothing I do could ever be boring or passé. And just like that, I got happy."

"You . . . stopped trying to prove it to anyone."

"Oh, the big joke on us all is that there's actually nothing to prove anyhow. You're only boring if *you* think you're boring."

"You . . . you think my work would be better if I focused on New York and stopped traveling?"

"I think your work would benefit from you doing whatever thrills you. And it doesn't matter what that thing is. If it's photos of knitting needles from here until you die, then you're still honoring yourself. It's not a concession if it gives you life."

". . . Florine . . . Ms. Weatherbell . . . if I get this book deal, is there any chance you'd be interested in being a creative editor for the project?"

"Absolutely not, that sounds terrible. Now, if Simona ever brings these cookies, we can eat and then I'll show you the jewelry. I know, I know, that's not what you came to photograph, but your insatiable curiosity is more interesting to me than your mission statement. So, let's get to the diamonds and pearls already."

Chapter Seventeen

Gwen

An hour and a half later I leave Florine's, dazed, churning, energized and enervated all at once. I've got a memory card full of photos of Florine and her collections. I'm almost certain I've just secured a book deal. And she's just simplified something I thought was extremely complicated. So now look! There I go! Living in peace!

Right.

Because . . . what good is knowing what you want if you still can't have it?

So maybe I've been making some things harder than they needed to be, i.e., if my family are all homebodies then I'm a world traveler and we can all just stay in our neat little categories and wave at a distance. Maybe that doesn't have to mean that I *never* make a life mostly in one place, right? And that realization makes my situation with New York a lot easier to handle.

But my situation with Sam?

The damn elevator won't come. I've been jamming the button for the last ten minutes and then finally a neighbor sticks her head out of her door.

"People moving in on the sixth floor, sweetie, the elevator's in use the rest of the evening."

And it just figures. The expected mode of transportation hasn't exactly been on the menu du jour.

Stairs it is.

I burst through the doorway to the stairwell and pound down, flight by flight. Every step is taking me back to earth. And I have no idea what to do when I get to said earth. Call Sam? Text him? Wait a nail-biting two hours and hope his date has wrapped up by then? And then what do I do? Just get his voice in my ear and hope I know what to say?

You can change your lifestyle and it doesn't have to change who you are, Florine insists.

But that doesn't change the fact that if I were to tell Sam everything . . .

The truth is, I have no idea what to say. And that's fine. Because he's on the other side of the borough, hopefully sipping drinks and sparking it up with everyone's favorite comeback story, Katie McConnick. I bet she has fifty In Case of Emergencies. All lining up, breathing against the glass, vying for their moment in the sun to support her through her most recent paper cut.

I emerge out into the lobby, nod goodnight to the doorman, and step out into the chilly spring night. Though the world was sun-warmed and trending green this afternoon, there's a hint of winter in the air now that the sun is down and the moon is high and bright. We're in that in-between place, caught in the middle of two seasons and it's so apt for my life right now I almost laugh-cry right there on Fifth Ave.

Do I really have a choice but to tell Sam everything? He deserves to know why I booted him out of my life after he did everything for me today. He deserves the whole story. He called himself a work in progress, and . . . if we're going to be friends then he deserves to know just how much work is progressing in my own brain. In my own heart.

I still have no idea what I'll say to him, but . . .

Go home. Call Sam. Tell him that you're sick of winter and ready for spring but that you're kind of a goblin person and might hiss in the sunlight for a little while. He should understand that that, at its core, is a hopeful message, right?

"Right. Just gotta tell him I'm a goblin person."

"Tell who you're a what?"

"Sam! Holy smokes, you startled me!"

"Sorry."

"Did you wait here this *entire* time?"

"Not the entire time, but long enough for the doorman to start glaring at me. I think he has it out for loafers. You are . . . a lot sweatier than I thought you'd be."

"Yeah, I just ran down fifteen flights of stairs. You are . . . a lot less sweaty than I thought you'd be. After all that biking."

"I changed clothes in Danny's car."

"You made it back to Danny's car!"

"Just in the nick of time. It's kind of a funny story, actually. I had to sell a cat to save my soul."

"What? Hey, wait, what happened with Katie? You're not on your date!"

"I didn't see her."

"You didn't go? Oh no."

"Don't worry. I didn't stand her up. I was able to get her number from my mother so that I could call her to cancel respectfully. She understood. And actually seemed pretty relieved."

"But your big catharsis! You missed your chance."

"Oh, jeez, my ridiculous catharsis. Don't worry, I got you your dang catharsis. And for the record, it wasn't that cathartic."

"What do you mean?"

"I told her. About my crush in high school. And that I

thought she was wonderful. And that . . . even though I couldn't come to our date, and won't be scheduling another, I just wanted her to know that someone out there, for a long time, thought she was the most lovely person in the world. I . . . think it went over well. She thanked me and told me that no one had said something like that to her in a long time. Then she wished me luck and we hung up."

"And that wasn't cathartic to you?! Good lord, you have high standards."

"No . . . I . . . That wasn't the particular catharsis I needed, I don't think."

"Hold on, wait, wait, wait. Brenda finally gave you Katie's number? What convinced her? I thought she'd needle you into the date if it was the last thing she did."

"Brenda and I . . . actually had a pretty intense heart to heart."

"Oh. Really?"

"Yeah. I think . . . I think we've both actually needed some space from one another. But didn't know how to get it. But yeah, I saved Danny's car, talked to my mom, talked to Katie and, here's the kicker, guess who's snoozing happily in the car?"

"You got to the kittens in time?!"

"I sure did. They're inoculated and cleared health-wise and ready for adoption. My mom actually wants one. And I texted Danny, who said he'd consider taking one. The tow truck driver wants the black and white one . . . long story. And then me, of course. I'll be taking the fourth. So we just have to find a home for the last—"

"I. Want. One."

"Wait! Why are you crying? Gwen? Are you all right?"

"I want one of the cats. The one with the pink nose. I want her. *I. Really. Want her.*"

"Okay. Of course you can have her. Why are you crying? Is

it figuring out how to get a cat-sitter when you're away? Because Carl will only take Garpy? Gwen, I'll take your cats when you're away. I promise we'll figure it out. You don't have to give anything up to—"

"No, you don't understand. I'm not saying I want the kitten with the pink nose *and* I want everything to stay the same. I'm saying that I want the kitten with the pink nose and I want everything to *change*."

"Oh. Okay, um."

"Do you know why I wanted that Florine Weatherbell interview so badly?"

"She's your hero. And if you got the interview, you'd get the book deal."

"And why did I want the book deal?"

"So that you'd have enough money to go to Portugal for a long time."

"See? I even fooled *you*! Figures, since I was so good at fooling myself."

"You . . . don't want to go to Portugal?"

"Of course I do! Who doesn't? But . . . Remember when you told me that when I talked about being so different from my family that I was reminding myself it was true? Well . . . maybe you're a little right about that. Maybe . . . there are things about their lives that I actually really want. But if I tried to get them and failed that would just make everything . . . Of course I wanted that money for travel, because I'm me, at my core, but also I think, somewhere in the back of my mind, when I thought about that big chunk of money, I was imagining all the things it could do for me *here*. I wasn't thinking about what adventures it could buy me a ticket to. I was secretly thinking about . . . getting a nicer apartment. Somewhere I'd actually want to spend time. And putting some money in the bank, so I wouldn't have to hustle quite so hard to keep myself afloat. And what it might be like to see all four NYC seasons in one year. And what if that money helped me to . . . rest a little bit?"

"I . . . didn't realize that's what you were hoping for."

"Me neither. Until about an hour ago when a very smart woman told me that I'm only boring if *I* think I'm boring, and that if I want to change my lifestyle that doesn't mean I have to change who I am."

"You're worried that if you set up shop in one place you'll lose something about yourself that you really like."

"Not just something. *Everything.* Who I am, how I live, how I define myself . . . Wendy. My bio mom. She was a traveler."

"I remember."

"I don't have much left to connect with her over. And it's always been how I explained who I am. I *love* my unique job. I love that I travel so much. I love my lifestyle. I love telling people what I do. But . . ."

"You're tired."

"*I'm so tired.*"

"You want to make some changes."

"I really think I do."

"You want a kitten with a pink nose."

"And I want to be there when she grows up to be a cat."

"I think that's really nice."

"Oh, don't look at me like that, Sam. With all that sweetness in your eyes. I . . . Please, I can't have you look at me like that."

"Should I . . . cover my eyes? Here. Is that better? Why shouldn't I look at you like this?"

"Because . . . you don't really know me. And I don't deserve to get looked at so sweetly."

"You mean because you're in such a state of change right now? Come on, gimme a little credit here. I can handle that. Besides, you're the one who gave me this."

"Gave you what? Oh, for goodness' sake, you can open your eyes."

"This."

"The marble."

"Mostly green with a little yellow at the bottom. It's scary to change, Gwen. I, until about noon today, was not a find-a-car, drive-a-stranger-to-Manhattan, bike-her-down-Fifth-Ave kind of guy. It kind of . . . hurts when your stripes change. I get it."

". . ."

"I could be someone who helps you through that change. Instead of, you know, someone who feels betrayed when you evolve and change with time. Or whatever it is that you're picturing being a dealbreaker for me at some point."

"No. Sam. That's not quite what I mean. Though, it is nice to hear you say that."

"What is it that you mean?"

"I . . . I—Oh, God."

". . ."

". . ."

"Okay, well, while you're figuring out how to say . . . whatever that is. Can I say something else?"

"I . . . sure."

"You know the big catharsis? The one that coming clean to Katie was supposed to give me?"

"Of course."

"Well, it was nice to be honest with her. But Gwen . . . it was the wrong catharsis, because it was the wrong conversation. Katie was not the person I was supposed to be coming clean to."

"Sam . . ."

"Gwen, you kinda knocked my socks off today. I like you. A lot. Do you . . . would you . . . wanna go on a date with me? One that doesn't involve sitting eighteen inches from a bus bathroom? Because, yeah, I think you're *great*. And even if you don't want to go on a date . . . I just . . . wanted you to know. And I wanted to say it. At least once."

"Urrrrghghghghgg."

"Um. Wow. Are you okay? That's not a reaction I was expecting."

"I . . . love . . . everything you just said to me. It's the best thing I've heard in so long. But . . . I waited too long. I'm such a chicken. URGHGHGHG. Sam, I have to tell you something."

"Yes. Shoot. Please."

"She's my *cousin*."

"Who?"

"The woman that George left your mom for. George's new girlfriend. Er. Wife. *That's* the big family event I was just at. My dad's family. It was for her wedding. *Their wedding*. The five-hundred-person wedding with all your mom's friends that she stayed home and felt humiliated over. I was there!"

"Gwen—"

"And I can tell you, for a fact, that he wasn't cheating on your mom. You know how I know? Because here's the real kicker. He met my cousin exactly eighty-four days ago. Well, eighty-five now. And I know that because . . . *I was the one who introduced them*. URGHGHGHGHG!!! Can you believe the destiny involved here? I just . . . I can't."

"Okay . . . um . . . I think you'll feel better if you explain?"

"Eighty-five days ago I was at a jeweler's in Boston. My friend's place. Shooting some of her stuff as a favor, so she could put the photos up on her website. And in walks this man. He wanted to get this old heirloom ring cleaned because he was going to finally propose to his partner. Your mom. Ughghg. And yeah, and he caught my eye because he was wearing these pretty substantial old class rings."

"George's rings. So intense."

"Right? Yeah. So we got to talking about them and I asked if I could interview him for my blog, and he said yes. I took the photos. And anyhow, while I was in Boston shooting the photos for the friend, I had made plans to also see my cousin because I hadn't seen her in a really long time. So, for the interview portion with George, I just had him come to the restaurant where I was meeting my cousin so I wouldn't have to scurry across town after the interview. Anyhow, he was still talking to me when my cousin showed up and I got to see sparks fly in real time. About three weeks later she sent me a photo of the heirloom ring on her own finger. Anyhow, it's all my fault and your mother will never forgive me. And I can't even begin to tell you how sorry I am and—*Why are you laughing at a time like this?*"

"Can I . . . Can I hug you for a minute?"

"I . . . yes. You can."

"Okay. So. Hi. That's better. Oh, you fit very nicely under my chin. Gwen, I just want to make one thing really, really clear. My mother is *happy* to be rid of George. I was just talking to her about that. She said, and I quote, 'I'm glad I know the real him now.' She understands that he is someone who was *always* capable of leaving her like that, she just didn't know that until recently. You didn't change who George was by innocently introducing him to your cousin. You helped show us the *real* George. That's all."

"But . . . But . . . Sam . . . What will your mother think? How could she ever look at me with clear eyes? I'll always be the woman who wrecked her seven-year relationship."

". . . Hey, can I borrow your hand for a second?"

"Huh?"

"I just need you to press this button here on my phone . . ."

"Um . . . What did I just purchase for you?"

"Plane tickets to New Orleans. I'm going on the trip, by the way, to the food festival. Thanks to you."

"Oh, *no*. Now your mother is *really* going to hate me. Not only did I destroy her relationship but I convinced you to leave the nest!"

"I told you before, Gwen. My mother loves anyone who is good for me. I told her I wanted to go on this trip, and that your enthusiasm was what gave me the push, and you know what? She was *excited* for me. Turns out, no one wants to feel like a dependent leech. Turns out, she wants me to be happy. Go figure. Also, she wants to go to Iceland, like you said. She even sent this text. See?"

"*See if your travel guide friend wants to go with us so we don't get lost and have all our money stolen.* She thinks I'm a travel guide?"

"There's a good chance she's still kinda confused about what your job is."

"Okay, okay, so she thinks I'm your friend who is encouraging you to get out and see the world. I get that she could take a shine to that. But how are we going to tell her about my cousin and George? That *really* seems like something I won't be able to come back from."

"Gwen. She already knows."

"What?!"

"I'm telling you. She sleuthed the crap out of you, recognized George from your blog post all those weeks back, figured out that you also follow the woman who he married. Sleuthed it down to the bottom and saw that you were cousins and even saw a post of hers thanking you for introducing them."

"What?!"

"Yeah. It's borderline weird and I'm going to tell her to stop spending so much time on the internet. But yeah. She actually already told me all about that an hour ago."

"She told you."

"Yup."

"About me."

"Uh huh."

"So, this whole story. You already knew it?"

"Yes."

"And you still came and waited for me outside Florine's house?"

"Absolutely."

"And . . . and . . . and . . . your mother . . . she's just *fine* with it?"

"*You're* not the person who married George. You're just related to her. And besides, I think . . . some sinister part of her brain is excited to have some insider info on George's relationship. I don't think she has high hopes for their future."

"Well, she can join the club on that one."

"See? You're already in a club with my mom. This is going great."

"Sam? I feel I should acknowledge that we've been hugging for a very long time."

"Yes. We have. Hey, so remember when I admitted my feelings for you?"

"Yes. I heard that part."

"Well, I guess I'd kind of like to know what you think? Is the whole George thing your main issue or . . .?"

"Um."

"Because I have a really big crush on you. I'm sure you've gathered. And I just wondered how you were feeling. On your end. Because people who only have friendly feelings for one another don't generally fret about whether their moms will like them, or hug for ten minutes on the street, or use each other's fingers to purchase plane tickets. So . . . if I've misread this please feel free to ask me to stop hugging you."

"No, no! Don't stop hugging. You know when I cried and said I wanted one of the kittens?"

"Just now? Yes. I recall."

"Well, I *do* actually want one of the kittens. But I was also talking about you, Sam. I mean . . . that I want the kind of life where I can have two cats and . . . a boyfriend. Yes, I want the cat with the pink nose. And . . . I want the boy with the blue hair. I really want you."

"Oh, *good*."

"I won't be an easy girlfriend, you know. Even if I set up shop here in NYC, I'm still going to be traveling a lot more than your average bear. I know you don't like long-distance dating."

"When did I say that?"

"You couldn't make it work with your girlfriend from Tacoma. Your escalator date."

"Oh. It wasn't the distance. We just . . . didn't like each other that much. I can do long distance. I can be flexible. And I'll come see you in interesting places too."

"You say it like it'll be easy."

"Is it ever easy to make your life match up with someone else's?"

"I . . . honestly don't know. I've never tried."

"I'm very good at trying. Seriously. You're going to be blown away with how good I am at trying."

"Well, I was there when you biked me up a hill, so I'm actually very familiar with how good you are at trying."

"I mean, don't you think that that's all you can really give someone? At the beginning at least?"

"The old college try?"

"Yeah."

"Hey, you waylaid Niles Shaw for me."

"Yeah . . . as I was leaving I stopped and looked back . . . I guess I just wanted to see you get all the way through the door. And then I saw him."

"You have your very own autograph now."

"Ha. Yeah. Here it is, on this old, stained receipt. Let's burn it."

"No way! I'm framing this and putting it on my wall. Oh, my God! Maybe I'll put a picture of it on IG and he can finally feel what it's like to get taunted by a rival."

"A rival who just secured a book deal, I might add."

"The book deal. I haven't even called Celeste yet. Oh my gosh, there's so much to think about. My head is spinning."

"Well . . . that makes sense. Considering the day we've had. We don't have to get it all figured out right this second, you know. We can figure it out little by little. We've got time."

"And chemistry."

"Lots of that. Do you . . . can I give you a ride home?"

"Sam. Come on."

"What?"

"Are you really going to take care of all those kittens by yourself tonight?"

"I mean . . . what are my options?"

"I'm coming with you."

"To my apartment?"

"Hey, Sam?"

"Yeah?"

"Let's go home."

Epilogue

"Oh, my GOD it's a whale. Did you SEE THE WHALE, IT'S A WHALE."

"Sam, I think there's a chance your mom is into whales."

"Yeah, I mean, I know she always liked fishing so I think the scale is just really blowing her mind right now."

"How many Brenda-and-the-whale pictures do you think I'm going to be obligated to take?"

"Judging from the Brenda-and-the-glacier experience yesterday, at least five hundred."

"Well, I'm all right with that. She's such a good subject."

"I love how much your followers have taken to her."

"Brenda's adventures really please the people."

"Old woman tries new things. Young woman goes along for the ride."

"Son-slash-boyfriend chimes in in the comments section . . . Hey, happy anniversary, by the way."

"You remembered!"

"Of course I remembered. You don't have to sound so surprised."

"You forgot last year."

"I was very busy last year planning that girls' weekend for you and your mom and Laura."

"Can you please not refer to it as a girls' weekend when I was one of the main ingredients?"

"You gave each other pedicures."

"That's not necessarily a gendered practice!"

"Hey. Not only did I remember our anniversary, I even got you a gift."

"You got me a gift!?"

"Yup."

"Oh, that's . . . that's a very small box."

"Open it."

"I'm . . . oh, boy."

"Be brave. Open it!"

"It's . . . a ring . . . for you? An . . . I don't want to say it and be wrong. But . . . this is an engagement ring, right? For you? That you're giving to me?"

"Yes. Your mom told me that you've . . . been wanting to ask, but since I don't wear jewelry you had no idea what to get me. So I picked one that made me think of you and that's your anniversary gift. I crossed a big old task off your list. And no pressure, by the way. You can give it to me whenever. I'm not expecting any specific timeline."

"You took care of it just like that, huh?"

"You know I try not to leave you hanging in the breeze."

"It's so pretty. And little. You better try it on, just to see if it fits."

"I can't try it on yet! Not until you give it to me."

"Just . . . Okay. You're right . . . Sorry. Got a little excited . . . The stone is blue."

"Indigo blue."

"Oh, come on, my hair hasn't been blue for, like, a year."

"Well, this color will always make me think of you."

"How about I dye it again for our wedding."

"Oh! Are we gonna have one of those?"

"Come on, it'll be an adventure."

"We tend to like those, don't we?"

"Wanna go have another one right now?"

"Always."

"Let's go."

Seatmate

CARA BASTONE

Dial Delights

Love Stories
for the
Open-Hearted

Keep reading for an exclusive sneak peek at Cara Bastone's new novel ***Through the Blue.***

Chapter One

A word on the color pink.

Sometimes you get to stand underneath a late-blooming cherry blossom tree at the tail end of a finally warm May, and vanilla-pink petals rain down on your outstretched hands like fragrant, feather-light rain, because you've just done the hard thing, the terrible thing, you've just returned the final box of your now ex-boyfriend's things, and he's walking away for the last time, down the block, you'd see him turn the corner if you looked, but you don't look, because there's a thunderstorm of seashell petals all around you and freedom has you turning your face to the blueberry sky and the sunshine, friends, paints you, warmly, with all the possibilities of a fresh new life.

By "you," I mean "me."

I'm under the cherry blossom tree. And long story short, I'm now the living embodiment of that one Nicole Kidman meme right after she divorced Tom Cruise.

Cue the George Michael ('90s version).

I am *free*.

"Hi, Soli!" a little voice calls to me, and I turn to see my landlord's six-year-old daughter skipping up to me on two mint green sneakers. She's got coppery hair, a bright red dress, and a carton of eggs carefully held between her two palms.

"Whatcha doin'?" she asks.

Whatcha doin' is probably the thing she's said the most in her entire life. I've never once met someone who cares more about what someone else is doin'.

"Embracing life," I tell her, both arms still up toward the sky.

"Everything all right?" my landlord asks as he approaches me warily. He's got a bag of groceries in each arm, filled to the brim, which explains why his kid is carrying eggs.

I nod and drop my arms. Something about having your landlord watch you embrace newfound freedom takes the fun out of it.

Ethan is normally a keep-to-himself sort of guy, and I've never gotten the impression that he likes me very much anyhow. Our building is a crumbling old townhouse right where Kensington bleeds into Windsor Terrace. I'm in the garden apartment; he's on the second floor with his daughter. He's got a backyard balcony and a wrought-iron staircase that winds down to said garden. I've got a stuck backdoor and occasional mice. One thing I can say about this guy, however, is that he never seems to get around to raising the rent. Once a month I forgive him almost every sin as I'm sending along that weak little Venmo.

And one thing I can say about Jonah, my ex, is that he didn't fight me even a little bit on who got to keep our mega-cheap apartment. He just put the ring back in his pocket and pulled his suitcase down from the closet. That was three weeks ago. He's been bleeding out his big departure shoebox by shoebox, but finally, there is nothing left of Jonah in my home.

"Was that Jonah down the block?" Ethan asks.

"Yeah."

Ethan and Jonah used to text each other all the time. They'd talk in the hallway outside our door. I'm assuming he's tempted to run down the block after him, begging him to stay.

When I told Ethan at the beginning of May that Jonah was moving out, I watched him attempt to remain placid, but surprise raced across his face, followed quickly by something that seemed an awful lot like dismay. "Are *you* staying?" he'd asked trepidatiously.

I'd given him a polite grimace. "Yes."

He'd nodded.

And that was the last time we spoke.

Until now, when Ethan clears his throat and shifts the grocery bags. We're half a block down from our building, and unless I make up a fake errand, now we have to walk the rest of the way together.

"I like your dress," Miriam says, utterly saving the day. She's fallen into step beside me.

"Of course you do," I tell her. "You have *impeccable* taste." Which she really does. Every time I compliment her outfit (genuinely), she informs me that *she* chose it. One time I saw them on the way to soccer practice and Ethan had stuffed her into workout gear. She was a narrow-eyed stormcloud, arms crossed over nylon. My kind of gal.

Ethan clears his throat again. "Is that kitchen cabinet still giving you trouble? Jonah said he was going to fix it . . ."

Jonah did not fix it. Jonah moved out instead.

He's taken my silence about the cabinet door as affirmation that, yes, the thing is a piece of crap held on only with duct tape and good will.

"Well, let me know a good time and I'll come fix it," he mumbles.

"Okay." Sure. He makes offers like these, but I've been living there for two years, and I can count the number of times my landlord has actually fixed a problem for me on one finger.

"Nights are easiest for me. Mornings I'm usually taking deliveries at the bar." He nods his head in the direction of the bar he owns, a few blocks away.

"You're at the bar nighttimes, too!" Miriam says, doing

hopscotch between sidewalk cracks and giving her eggs a brief brush with death. She's walking backward now, talking to me. She looks around and then lowers her voice to a high whisper. "Sometimes he makes me a floor bed at the bar when he's really busy."

"Mimi!" Ethan is exasperated. "Even if you whisper, it's still telling the secret!" He quickly turns to me. "A floor bed in my *private office* at the bar. She's not out, like, with the patrons."

I'm holding up two hands. "Your business, not mine."

He's going to say more. Insist, I'm sure, on how comfortable this floor bed is, but instead he breaks off and furrows his brow. He's staring in the direction of our townhouse. I follow his gaze and see a very large man sitting on our wide steps. He's got a beanie pulled down almost to his eyes, despite the warm weather, and his elbows are on his knees. I can hear the pew pews of some shooting game on his phone.

"You expecting someone?" he asks me. He's trying to figure out if he's going to have to play bouncer.

"Definitely not." I haven't even had any friends over since Jonah and I broke up. I've been enjoying the pantsless solitude with every ounce of my being.

"Okay." Ethan shifts the grocery bags and steps in front of me and Miriam. "Excuse me," he calls.

The man looks up and then immediately stands, shoving his phone in his back pocket. He's looking right past Ethan. He's staring at me. There's something vaguely familiar—

"Aunt Soli."

I gape at him. There's only one person on earth who'd call me that and . . . Oh, my God. This person is not a man, he's a *kid.* Just passed his eighteenth birthday last month, if I've been keeping track correctly.

"*Cody?*"

He seems really relieved that I've recognized him.

But the truth is, I haven't. I'm scrambling through context clues.

I step around Ethan and the kid bounds down the stairs to meet me. He pulls up short when I take a step back from him. Because he's well over six feet tall and extremely broad in the shoulder. I'm searching for that vague familiarity I first spotted, struggling to see it now. I guess I see a loose family resemblance, but he is built like a Hummer, and my brother is more like a mid-size sedan.

"You . . ." I say, squinting and stepping toward him. "Are enormous."

He grimaces. "Yeah."

"Sorry to do this, kid, but I think I need to see some ID." Look, I'm a hot early-thirties gal living alone. If I swing open my door for this person, no questions asked, that has Netflix limited series documentary written all over it.

Ethan, meanwhile, is looking back and forth between us. He sets the groceries down, hands Miriam the keys, and shoos her up the steps.

The kid digs through his wallet and then hands me two things. One is a driver's license with the name Cody Henrik Beck in bold letters. The other is his phone, showing my brother's Facebook. (Something I haven't looked at in over a decade.) There's a photo album called *Cody.* I thumb through it as fast as possible, trying to ignore details and the searing pain of watching my nephew grow at light speed. I go from the kindergartener I remember vividly to the nearly grown man standing in front of me in ten seconds flat.

I hand everything back to him and walk up two of my front steps. Then I turn and hold my arms out to him, so that we can hug without him having to basically take a knee. I'm humbled when he walks directly into my arms.

"Hi," I say with a squeeze. "Sorry I didn't recognize you."

"That's okay," he says. "I sort of didn't recognize you either."

"Well. Come inside, then."

I head up the stairs and catch the door behind Miriam, who is scampering up the wooden stairs to their apartment on the second floor. I hold open the front door for Cody, but he and Ethan are standing on the top step next to each other.

"I'm Ethan, the landlord. I live upstairs." He holds his hand out to Cody for a shake.

Cody shakes hands tentatively, because he's a teenager. He probably daps more often than he shakes. But maybe he's tentative because he's also just gotten his first good look at Ethan. Who has a very interesting face. One your eyes might snag on if you haven't gotten used to it. He has raised scarring all along the left cheek, from his jaw all the way up, in cursive around his brow bone and over his forehead. It glows against his coloring, lavenders and mauves in a mapped pattern all the way up into his copper hairline.

He often wears a surgical mask and a baseball cap, probably because he gets sick of people gaping at him, the way my nephew is right this second.

"Come in, Cody."

He starts and drops Ethan's hand and scurries in after me.

I unlock my first-floor apartment door and do the Vanna White hands, so that Cody will go inside already.

Right as I'm about to follow him though, there's a gentle tap to my shoulder.

I turn and there's Ethan with the groceries. He still hasn't gone upstairs.

"If you need anything," he says with a glance toward my open apartment door. "Come get me. I'm here all night."

I flash him the thumbs up and join Cody in my apartment who, for the second time in less than a minute, is gaping.

Okay, fine, it's probably overwhelming in here. The front room (with all the good south-facing light) is my workroom and storage area for my job. Which means that every square inch is covered in swatches and bolts upon bolts of fabric. Four different sewing machines, canvases painted in every color combination under the sun, mannequins wearing togas, half-finished stained-glass windows propped up, and rugs overlapping rugs overlapping rugs. It is a joyful, drunken, chaotic kegger of color. And it is, in short, exactly what it feels like to step directly into my brain.

"This is . . . your apartment?" he asks dimly.

"This is my office," I clarify. Which, based on the expression on his face, clarifies nothing. I wave him through the caster doors to the rest of my place.

"What's your job?"

"I'm a textile designer." He's still looking concerned and overwhelmed by the bird's nest of color he's just endured. "A successful one," I reassure him. "Mostly for interiors. But I take on the odd fashion project here and there."

We're through the dim walk-through living room to the kitchen now, which boasts a microscopic two-top underneath a slitted eye of a window. I press him into a chair that disappears underneath his bulk.

"So . . ." I prompt.

His shoulders are rounded forward, and he scratches at his beanie. He's trying to make himself blend in, I think. Which is, frankly, not possible against the wallpaper (ballet dancers in various positions, designed by yours truly, of course).

He's not replying yet. I'm losing patience.

"Cody." I've foregone everything but studying him, my chin propped on my hand. "Why are you here?"

He winces without actually moving a single muscle. I immediately feel I've stepped on a kitten's tail.

"I mean, I'm not complaining!" I rush. "But I'm definitely surprised."

"I'm in the city for a couple months. Before school starts."

"Oh! Wow! School . . ." This was his senior year of high school, which means he must be headed to . . .

"Duke," he says with an unmistakable frown. "I graduated a semester early. Mostly so that I could go to this training camp thing in the city." He's glancing at me and then away. The specter of my brother is rising up between us. Cody was *glued* to Flynn's hip when he was a kid. Flynn fielded every question headed his way. I'm starting to get the impression that that hasn't changed much over the years. It's almost like Cody is waiting for someone else to come along and explain why the hell he's sitting in my kitchen right now.

"What kind of training camp?"

"It's for athletes. One-on-one skill building."

I'm grimacing because I have a feeling this next question is going to shine a very bright light on just how removed from his life I've been. "And . . . what sport are you playing these days?"

"Oh. Uh. Basketball. For Duke."

"That . . . sounds like a big deal!"

We're smiling weakly at each other.

"Yeah . . ." He's glancing down now, and I follow his gaze. There's a large backpack at his feet that I haven't clocked until now. Probably because it was attached to the enormous beloved I still can't believe is sitting at my breakfast table. "Well . . ." he says eventually. "There's kind of this one week . . . break . . . for the camp. And you're allowed to stay at the facilities. But . . . they kind of suck . . . and I guess I was just wondering . . ."

"You want to stay with me?"

Big blue eyes, a beanie adjustment, and a half hopeful, half embarrassed shrug. "If that's . . . okay."

"Well," I say as I stand. "Let's see if you'll even fit in the guest room."

He gives a surprised laugh, but I wasn't joking. My quote unquote guest room is actually what was once a mudroom off the side of the kitchen. It's not much larger than a closet, with a stuck backdoor to the backyard that has exclusive use by Ethan and Miriam. Figuring we were never going to use it for its intended use when Jonah and I moved in, we threw a little daybed and a lamp and a humidifier in there for when his mother came to visit.

"It's great," Cody says immediately. He's already slid past me and set his backpack down. He's crouching slightly to skirt under the light fixture that sways precariously overhead.

"I guess it'll do for a week," I say with a shrug.

He's not looking at me.

"Are you busy for your break? Have anything planned?" I ask.

He shakes his head.

"Okay. Well . . ." It strikes me that it's five o clock on a Friday night and it's warm outside in New York Fuckin' City. But he's sitting on the bed, looking completely immovable. I say the only thing that comes to mind. "Pizza?"

And, *finally,* he smiles at me.

***

He ate all the pizza. Except for the slice and a half I was able to snag. And then he broke down the pizza box. And then he took out the trash and the recycling. And then he went back to his sad little pantry and closed the door and now I'm lying on my bed with one wall between us, staring at the ceiling.

He broke down the pizza box without me having to ask him. Which means he's got some savvy. But still . . . he's a kid and I have no idea what to do with him.

Is offering him a tiny bed and a large pizza enough? Does he need cash as well? I haven't budgeted for that, obviously, but it should be okay, depending on how much one kid needs to survive for seven days. But I know there's something else I really *should* do.

I open my phone and find my brother in my contacts. My thumb hesitates, which is ridiculous because *your kid showed up on my doorstep* is a perfectly good reason to call. I'm sweating. It's a sad state of affairs that I need a "good reason" to call my brother in in the first place, but here we are.

I abruptly chicken out and instead decide to text him.

Hi, I know it's been a long time, I type.

No, too stilted. I delete it and try again.

Hey, dude. Long time no—God! No. Way too casual. He's not a former classmate I happened to run into in a bus station. He's my estranged big brother.

Maybe I should just address the elephant in the room? Okay . . . how about something like: Flynn. Did I lose you by degrees or did you finally just take Mom and Dad's side? I knew that was probably inevitable since you still live there and I've been gone for so long but still, I didn't think—NO! No. It's sort of cathartic to see it typed out like that but, of course, these are not the sort of issues one addresses (or solves) over text. And this isn't about me. This is about Cody. Better to keep it simple.

Hi. I'm putting up Cody while he's on break from camp. Just thought you should know. Hope you're well. Call if you need anything.

I blink in confusion when the text gets delivered in green. My brother has always used iPhones so . . . A quick google confirms what my roiling stomach already knows. He has most likely blocked me.

I try to think of the last time I contacted him. The sad truth is I could have been blocked for a few years and I wouldn't have even known.

Right! So! Right. Technically nothing is different than it was ten minutes ago. I was blocked then and I'm blocked now.

The only upside to getting kicked out and cut off from your parents as a teenager is that it makes you fairly numb to lesser levels of abandonment.

So . . . Cody. Right. The matter at hand: Soli Beck is the sole Beck who happens to know his current whereabouts. But . . . *someone* else should know, right? Circle of accountability and all? What if I fall into an open manhole? Who would buy him pizza?

I pull on some pajama pants and tiptoe past Cody's door and out through my office. I scamper quickly up the wooden stairs to Ethan's apartment and give it the ol' knock knock without another second thought.

Twenty seconds later, the door opens and Ethan is still tugging on a T-shirt. I get a half-second glimpse of his bare stomach.

"Everything all right?" he asks in a low voice. He's scrubbing one hand over his eyes.

Oh. I've never heard his I-was-just-sleeping voice before. I'm reminded of thunder in the distance, with undertones of lion.

"Sorry, did I wake you?" It's only 9:15.

"No, no. It's fine. I fell asleep in front of the TV. What's up?"

"Oh. I just wanted to . . ." Wait, why *am* I telling him this in person? Why the hell didn't I text him this? I clear my throat and put on my newscaster voice (in order to sound official). "I just wanted to let you know that Cody is going to be staying with me for a little while." I flail a little. "About a week. You're the landlord, so I thought . . . you should know . . ."

He's looking confused. "You don't have to report guests to me."

"Right." I'm stymied. "Nice pants, by the way."

"Oh." He jolts and looks down at his pajama pants. "They were a gift. Miriam. I don't usually—oh."

He's glanced at my pajama pants and realized that he's wearing Ponyo and I'm wearing Totoro. We match. Adjacently, at least.

"She's got good taste," I tell him for the hundredth time.

"Is she sleeping?" I ask.

"Probably by now. But she's back at her mom's. We switch on Friday evenings."

"Oh, right. I think I knew that already. Anyway. Thanks for the help today." I point down toward Cody. Aka, the hulking stranger Ethan put his grocery bags in front of.

"Is he visiting? From out of town?" Ethan asks.

"Sort of. He's in the city for a little bit and needed a place to crash."

"Got it."

"I'd offer you some pizza, but he ate it all." I don't know why I'm telling him this. Other than the fact that it's been my life's goal to never take care of a child and now there's a two-hundred-pound one sleeping in my mudroom.

Ethan laughs and correctly interprets my bemusement. "Let's see . . . it's May and he's visiting New York. Take him to a Brooklyn Cyclones game."

I salute him. "Thanks."

"And there will be a taco truck at the bar for the next few days. A pop-up kitchen sort of thing. He can eat for free."

I put my hands on my hips. "What about me?"

He quirks his face. "You can always eat and drink for free. Everything at the bar is free for you."

"What? Since when?"

"Since always? I told Jonah . . ." he trails off and scratches at the back of his neck. Because obviously Jonah never told me.

I'm appalled at all the free drinks I've missed out on. It's not the *drinks* part that I'm drawn to. It's the *free* part. Even now in my financially stable thirties, if something is free, I'm partaking.

"Expect to see me there every night from here on out."

His eyes round. He may have bitten off more than he can chew. He clears his throat. "Um. Well, if you're all good . . ."

"Yes. I am. See you soon." I give a grateful little wave.

Three minutes later, I'm crawling back into bed, extremely relieved that at the very least, Ethan's got my back.

COURTESY OF AUTUMN LAYNE PHOTOGRAPHY

CARA BASTONE is the bestselling author of *Ready or Not, Promise Me Sunshine,* and *No Matter What.* She lives and writes in Brooklyn with her husband, sons, and an almost-goldendoodle. Her goal with her work is to find the swoon in ordinary love stories. She's been a fan of the romance genre since she found a grocery bag filled with her grandmother's old Harlequin Romances when she was in high school. She's a fangirl for pretzel sticks, long walks through Prospect Park, and love stories featuring men who aren't hobbled by their own masculinity.

carabastone.com
Instagram @carabastone

Discover more books by

CARA BASTONE

Available wherever books are sold